The Peppermint Lodge

THE PEPPERMINT LODGE

A SINGLE PARENT ROMANCE (LARGE PRINT EDITION)

HOCKEY SWEETHEARTS
BOOK FOUR

JEAN ORAM

The Peppermint Lodge

A Single Parent Sweet Romance

A Hockey Sweethearts Novel
By Jean Oram

© 2023 Jean Oram
All rights reserved
First Edition 2023
Large Print Edition

Cover design by Jean Oram

Complete cataloguing information available online or upon request.

Oram, Jean.

The Peppermint Lodge: A Single Parent Sweet Romance / Jean Oram.—1st. ed.

ISBN: 978-1-990833-45-8, 978-1-990833-46-5 (paperback), 978-1-990833-47-2 (large print), 978-1-989359-73-0 (ebook).

First Oram Productions Large Print Edition: April 2023

CHAPTER 1

May

Maybe taking Rylnn to a Mother's Day dance wasn't such a brilliant idea, after all. His four-year-old was literally dancing him off his feet. And Landon Jackson was a darn good dancer.

But keeping up with his daughter, dressed as a princess? That was going to end him.

"Rylnn, I need to sit." His ankle, which had been shattered during a hockey game, nearly ending his pro career, was telling him it was done being held captive in cowboy boots and trying to bust a move like he was still in his twenties.

Rylnn crossed her arms and made her big brown eyes even bigger.

"Ry, I need a break."

She harrumphed with her entire body.

"Just one song." He grabbed a nearby chair and spun it under him. Sweetheart Creek's community center had a generous dance floor filled with mothers and sons, as well as some fathers and daughters, and pretty much all of the rest of the small town. There was air-conditioning, but it was struggling to keep up with the throng of dancers filling the old, converted barn. Chances were, despite his physical conditioning, his cheeks were a burning red, and if not, they certainly felt like it. Coach Louis should have the team try to keep up with his daughter on the dance floor as part of their dryland training.

As Landon pulled off his cowboy hat to fan himself, he caught the eye of a gorgeous woman he'd been noticing all night. She was tall, and not what he'd call dolled up. Yet she had a freshness about her, an effortless air he found instantly attractive. Currently, she was trying to mask a smile, no doubt brought on by his obvious inability to keep up with his preschooler.

"One song," he repeated, as Rylnn tried to tug him back onto his feet, her unruly spray of black curls waving under her tiara.

When he refused to budge, her eyes brimmed with tears and her lower lip stuck out, then trembled. He could have sworn the nanny had been giving her lessons in acting helpless, as well as how to pull on his heartstrings.

What was he supposed to do? The world wasn't gentle with women who couldn't take care of themselves, and that was not the kind of woman he wanted to raise.

Was he coddling Ry? Was the nanny? His little girl needed to go outside and get grubby and learn by doing—which apparently was difficult while living in downtown San Antonio.

Despite his repeated demands that the nanny take Rylnn outside to play, her clothes were never grass-stained. No dirt smudges. No holes in her wardrobe. No character-building scratches or bruises from testing her limits in the playground. No mud falling off her cute little sneakers.

Rylnn's face was turning a dark brown-red, the change subtle but alarming.

Landon sat straighter, panic and pre-emptive humiliation burning through him. "No. No, no, no. Don't cry." He reached out as if there was a magical button he could tap to prevent the impending meltdown.

Had her mother never said no to her? No, he'd seen Zofia establish boundaries the times he'd visited them in Hawaii, before Zofia had passed away. Was it grief? Little-girl sorrow? Too many changes in her life over the past year wearing down her resiliency?

As Rylnn tipped her head back to let out a giant wail—which would no doubt tell everyone in the small community just how out of his depth he was with fatherhood—the gorgeous cowgirl he'd been eyeing crouched beside his daughter.

"You are the most beautiful princess I've ever seen." The woman's tanned face was kind, the compliment sounding so genuine it made a lump form in Landon's throat as Rylnn blinked in surprise.

"Are these real jewels?" She fingered the pink, glittery skirt of Rylnn's dress.

Wordlessly, Rylnn shook her head.

The woman studied Rylnn's tiara. "Did you know my friend April was a rodeo princess? But I don't think she ever once got a crown as lovely as yours."

"It's a tiara."

"Oh, that's right. Tiara. A crown goes all the way around, doesn't it?"

Rylnn nodded, chin tipped down, shyly taking in her admirer. This close, Landon could see the woman had freckles across the bridge of her cute nose. Landon was a sucker for freckles, as well as height. And, actually, pretty much anyone who could prevent an embarrassing, public meltdown. This woman could've asked him for a Ferrari right now and he would have signed the check. Happily.

"I saw you twirling earlier. I wish my dress did that."

Rylnn, now completely distracted, put one hand on her hip and tipped her head to the side in a move that reminded Landon of Zofia. It made him miss his best friend and the strong mother Ry would be unlikely to remember.

"You're not wearing a dress," Rylnn pointed out.

The woman looked down at her jeans, cowboy boots and flannel shirt. "True. Too much of a cowgirl, I suppose." She stood with a laugh, her smile wide, not quite hiding subtle lines of fatigue. "What I should say is that I wish I had a dress like yours." She shrugged easily. "I don't really have dresses anymore."

"Really?" Rylnn was staring at her as though she'd just admitted she liked how worms tasted.

"Nowhere to wear them, I guess."

His daughter's frown deepened.

Landon tried to imagine the woman in a dress that was feminine and clingy. She'd be a knockout. Slender curves, long legs, and those eyes that were kind, yet mischievous, giving her a sexy, illusive air. Too bad he didn't have time for a girlfriend, or he'd ask for her number.

Landon's friend and teammate Maverick Blades joined them, saying, "Hey, I'm heading out."

Landon shook his head. Maverick had coaxed him here, saying it would be good for Rylnn. Bonding and such. He'd expected Mav to stay as long as he did, if for no other reason than to lend moral support.

"Please stay," he said too quickly.

So much for looking cool and in control for this cowgirl babe. Although, when it came to parenthood, he was discovering he wasn't too proud to beg.

"Dude, there's no reason for me to be here now that my own mom's left for the night," Maverick said with a laugh. He nodded to the woman chatting with Rylnn. "Hey, Cass. How's it going?"

"Hey."

"Cass?" Landon stood. He hoped he didn't wince as his ankle bit him, sending a shard of pain up his calf.

Maverick gave him a stern look. "Next season starts soon enough. Take care of that ankle, Blockade."

"Yes, honey," Landon said sweetly, earning a smirk from his friend.

Their regular season had just ended and he had a few months to recuperate before hitting the ice again. Plenty of time to finish healing.

Maverick tipped his cowboy hat to Cass and Rylnn, then headed toward the doors.

Abandoned. Some friend.

"I'm Landon." He offered his hand to Cass. She shook it firmly, her eyes assessing him.

"Dragons?" she asked, referring to the NHL San Antonio Dragons, the local pro hockey team that both he and Maverick played for.

"Goalie," he said. One of the most important positions on the team. Not that they had a decent defense, which meant he allowed way too many pucks past him to make him happy. Or to make him look good. He felt like he no longer deserved his nickname, The Blockade.

"And is this your daughter?" Cass asked, gesturing to Rylnn, who was now doing little twirls near a pale-looking boy who was slightly taller than she was.

"Yeah," Landon said. "This is Rylnn."

"My name is Cassandra, but everybody calls me Cass." She crouched down to talk to Rylnn. "And this is my son, Dusty. He's my date tonight."

Dusty, in his cowboy hat and jeans, gave Rylnn's hand a very serious shake. Rylnn curtsied and said something that sounded princessy. Landon really hoped this was a normal phase of childhood and not the beginnings of a personality disorder. Dusty looked confused, until another boy in a cowboy hat tugged him away with promises of a monster truck battle.

A two-step started, and the DJ's voice boomed through the room. "The next dance is for the moms out there. Kids, take your mothers onto the floor." There was a pause before the DJ singled out one of the grown men along the sidelines. "You, too, Ryan. Show Maria you appreciate the hours she's put into keeping you in line. Carly, give him a push, would you?"

The crowd laughed as a woman with curls as wild as Rylnn's obliged and gave her man a nudge toward what must be his mother.

Landon glanced back at Rylnn. Her eyes had

turned huge again, and her bottom lip was quivering.

Landon's heart squeezed.

Take your mothers onto the floor...

He had his arms out to sweep her into a hug, but before he knew it, Cass was intercepting his daughter, drawing her onto the floor and asking to be shown some princess dance moves. As Landon sank back in his seat and rested his ankle, he decided this Cassandra must be an angel sent from above.

* * *

When the song ended, Cassandra McTavish returned Rylnn to Landon. The kid was adorable and so full of energy it made her long for a daughter of her own. Even though Rylnn was way more girlie than she'd ever been allowed to be as a child, in some ways, she made more sense than her son did.

Dusty was a tried-and-true cowboy, ready to rub dirt in his wounds. And while she loved that about him, it didn't mean she always understood him and his adoration of all things cars and trucks.

Sometimes it would be nice to live with

someone who understood the joy that impractical, pretty things brought a woman.

Landon was sitting on one of the fold-up chairs far away from the DJ's stage, his elbows resting on his knees as he listened to Dusty, who'd wandered back to him. His longish wavy dark hair brushed the collar of his pale gray button-up shirt and he was listening so intently that Cass's heart pleaded with her brain to let it crush on someone—*him* in particular.

Ha. That was a big fat no, thank you. She'd tried the whole love thing and the only good part about it was that she now had Dusty.

When you had a husband, your sister shouldn't have to drop everything and fly across the country to help you through something difficult. Your husband should step up, right? But he hadn't. So if that was what love looked like, then no thanks. She didn't need it.

"Hello, boys," she said, taking the chair beside Landon. Rylnn crawled onto her dad's lap, half burying him in glittery pink tulle.

"Dusty was telling me about monster trucks." Landon gave Cass a smile that melted her heart. He didn't look like he wanted to be anywhere else than sitting with her son and talking about machines.

"Landon had a 4x4 with really big tires," her five-year-old said, his brown eyes huge.

"Wow. Really?"

"Do you like my shoes?" Rylnn asked, kicking one foot out so the guys could admire her footwear.

They looked, then went back to their conversation about 4x4s.

"They're very pretty," Cass said. "I like how they match your dress."

"I know. They're both pink."

"Does anyone want punch?" Cass asked.

"No, thank you," Dusty said.

"I do!" Rylnn exclaimed. "Pink punch!"

"Manners, Ry," Landon reminded her.

"Please."

Cass glanced at Landon to make sure it was okay, and he gave a small nod. She smiled, feeling ridiculously thrilled by the way his gray eyes held hers for a moment. It wasn't anything special, but it *felt* like it was, though there was no reason it should feel tingly and good. He probably looked at anyone and everyone with that slow, deep glimmer, like he actually saw the person in front of him.

"Do you want some?" she asked him.

"No, thanks," he murmured, with another

deep, thoughtful glance that made her insides go warm.

That man made her want to dream of families and true love.

She shook her head, tamping down the dream, and its dear friend, hope. Neither hopes nor dreams—at least the romantic kind—were a good use of her time. Her ex-husband, Archer, had become emotionally and physically absent when she'd needed him most, and had she seen him since?

Twice in the past five years.

Sure, she knew not every relationship sucked like hers had, but she had little hope that she'd find someone who might match and complement her independent ways.

Friends were better. Much better.

She marched to the punch table and surveyed the sugary drinks. And anyway, she *had* family and love. In fact, she'd moved all the way from Montana to Texas to live on the expanse of land next to her sister and brother-in-law. Family for her and Dusty.

And yeah, Cash and Alexa were busy building up their ranch and didn't have as much time to play a role in Dusty's upbringing as she may have expected, but what had she thought would happen? That they'd drop everything and restructure their lives around the two of them?

They had, in many ways, but Cass needed more.

She sighed, then realized Rylnn was at her elbow, having followed her across the barn.

"Pink punch," the little girl repeated.

"That shouldn't be a problem." Cass moved an almost-empty pitcher closer to her. "Pink punch to match your dress. You pour that one, and I'll pour the orange."

The four-year-old hesitated, then sloshed some liquid into her plastic glass. Cass caught the cup as it tipped, ensuring it didn't spill, while Rylnn set the pitcher back on the table with a clunk.

"Well done."

Rylnn looked pleased with herself, and they carefully carried their drinks across the bustling barn.

Dusty and Landon were still talking trucks.

"I poured it myself, Daddy!"

"Did you? Wow. Good job." He looked at Cass as if she'd helped his daughter solve a significant problem, such as world hunger.

"Do you like trucks?" Cass asked Rylnn, once they were settled with their drinks.

She shook her head. "Daddy used to have a truck. Now we drive a soovie."

"The SUV is, uh, easier," Landon said, wincing as if he knew trading in your truck in Texas Hill Country would get you heavily judged.

And it would.

"Oh, uh…" Landon reached out, using his sleeve to swipe at a dribble of punch on Rylnn's chin.

"Daddy," she complained, waving him away and nearly spilling her punch.

Cass got the feeling Landon was new to parenting, and she was curious about that. He was a natural, his obvious kindness and patience both winning traits. But he was awkward and slightly hesitant, too, as though afraid of getting it wrong.

It made her want to pull out her phone and do a quick online search to see if she could scrounge up some dirt about him and his personal life. Single? Divorced? A secret daughter who'd recently been pushed into his arms?

Cass suspected the first and last were the ticket. He didn't strike her as a divorcé.

"My mom drives a truck," Dusty said. "It's Auntie Lexa's 'cause ours got broken by a deer."

"We live in an old hunting lodge. It used to be called Buck Lodge, but I've renamed it," Cass said, gesturing in the direction of their home. Her heart lifted at the thought of the giant building, its new name, The Peppermint Lodge, its barn and pretty pond set out back. It was going to make a beautiful venue for brides and grooms to commit to each other. But it was going to take an enormous amount of work to bring the rustic, run-down and outdated buildings close to the charmingly romantic vision she carried in her imagination. "Having a truck comes in handy."

"It's not a 4x4. Uncle Cash says that old dinosaur runs on prayers."

Cass fought a smile. "Hey, are you calling Auntie Alexa's truck old? Because it's paid for." She gave Dusty a pretend frown, and Landon laughed.

"Never knock a woman's wheels," he advised.

"Thank you. You might offer other helpful life advice, such as—" she leaned forward dramatically "—your mom is always right." She winked at Dusty, and he gave her a funny little scowl from under his white cowboy hat.

Landon chuckled at their shenanigans and she felt warmed, a reminder that while she and Dusty might not be a traditional family, they were content and fortunate, their home filled with love.

"Keep your mom and your grandmas—if you

have them—happy and you'll probably live to see adulthood," Landon said.

Cass laughed. "Truth."

"Do you like Batman?" Dusty interjected, changing the subject.

"Enough life advice?" Landon grinned, causing the skin around his eyes to crinkle in the most delightful way. He was handsome. Not that grab-you-by-the-throat-and-shake-you kind of handsome, but something even more breathtaking, because his personality matched his good-looking exterior.

"I like Cinderella." Rylnn twirled, spilling punch down her dress. "Tonight is the ball!" She continued to spin, lost in her fantasy world, until Landon plucked her cup from her grasp.

"Do you like Batman?" Dusty insisted.

"Dusty…" Cass warned, willing her son to be patient and not so demanding.

"I do." Landon was thoughtful for a moment. "But I think Spiderman is my favorite. How about you? Batman or Spiderman?"

Dusty hesitated, and Cass waited to see what he'd say. He was a huge Batman fan. Like, the biggest. He always played Batman with her friend Hannah's son, and would ask for Thomas's Batmobile when they visited.

"Batman," Dusty said with a serious nod, causing Landon to laugh. "But Spiderman is okay." He pretended to shoot webs from his wrists.

Rylnn wiggled her way onto the chair next to her dad. "I'm a super princess. I have magical powers."

"What are your powers?" Cass asked.

"I'm magic."

A dance-off between parents and kids was announced, and Cass glanced at Rylnn to see if she'd heard. The girl's eyes went round and she popped off her chair, snatching her punch from her dad and downing the last of it.

"Daddy, no more breaks!"

"Boys?" Cass asked, when Dusty and Landon remained seated. She stood as well. "Up for a dance-off?"

"No. I'm staying with Landon." Dusty kept his focus locked on the hockey player. The boy needed a father figure something fierce. He adored his uncle Cash and the hired hand, Nick, but it wasn't the same as having a dad around full-time.

Landon turned to him. "How about it? Boys against girls?"

Dusty grinned.

"Hey, it's supposed to be parents against kids," Cass protested, trailing after them as they hurried onto the dance floor.

Soon the four of them were a mess of flailing arms and legs as they tried to keep up with the remix playing through the barn's speakers. "The Twist," spliced with "Jump Around," "YMCA" and about ten other songs were jammed into two minutes.

Rylnn was moving like she had made the remix herself, effortlessly flowing between different dances.

"Wow," Cass exclaimed. "Do you go to dance classes? You're really good."

Landon spread out his arms as if he loved the idea. "Is there such a thing as this—unstructured and fun, but in a dance class?"

"Probably." She glanced at Dusty. He seemed to be flagging, lacking his usual jam. He'd never been a super exuberant kid, but lately it was as though he'd been fighting a never-ending, low-grade bug.

"You okay?" she asked, touching his shoulder.

"I'm tired." He sat down on the floor, letting out a long sigh.

"How about you go sip some more of your punch?"

It looked like it was time to go back to the doctor and demand more tests, because something wasn't right.

Cass guided him off the dance floor as the songs ended, looking back, her gaze lingering on Landon's wide shoulders and happy smile. For a moment she allowed herself to imagine what it might be like if the four of them were a family.

CHAPTER 2

October (5 months later)

Landon scooped up his daughter and told Maverick he was doing a coffee run. Dylan O'Neill, the team's center, narrowed his eyes.

"Dude, you trying to weasel out of crawling under that sink again?" Dylan waved one of his crutches at the dusty, dark cabinet that reeked of mildew and old house.

Landon had spent at least an hour and a half in that small space with a cutting torch, breathing fumes, plus dealing with heat and muscle cramps, while he removed the ancient copper piping. Why Maverick didn't just gut the kitchen like he had most of the other rooms was beyond Landon. The century-old farmhouse was a money pit, so what was another fifty grand?

Then again, Landon suspected that Maverick's energy for ripping things out was fueled by his anger at being misrepresented in the press—and being force-traded as a result of his new less-than-stellar reputation.

Landon tossed the leather work gloves he'd been wearing Dylan's way. "Make yourself useful."

The man let out a huff. "You know I'd put in the new pipes if I wasn't in this cast."

"You'd think it was on your hand, not your foot."

He set the wrench and pipe he'd given Rylnn to "work on" off to the side, before hustling her out of the house so he didn't get roped into another job.

The reno site wasn't the best place for her, but over the summer they'd exhausted the local zoo, playgrounds, swimming pool and everything semi-kid-friendly that San Antonio had to offer. His daughter wasn't into sports, which meant purchasing baseball, football or basketball tickets were a waste, and there were only so many tea parties he could handle.

He was trying to limit her screen time, but now that his hockey season had started he was busier and more tired, and he could see the slippery slope trying to drag him downward. What was an extra movie each morning when he'd been up late at a game? What was an extra hour of TV when he had calls to return to his agent and trainer?

The season had only just begun and he was already worn-out, hoping the team didn't make play-offs so their season didn't stretch beyond April and into June.

Maybe he shouldn't be so determined to take over the nanny's duties when he was home.

Accept the help. Carve out more time for himself.

Like that was going to happen.

Kids needed their parents. Not some paid stand-in. And that gum-smacking, phone-addicted twenty-something was going to warp his little girl even if she was the best the agency had at the moment.

Hence, here he was, teaching her the difference between a wrench and a hammer while helping Maverick work on his old farmhouse, so they didn't get lured down the easy path of too much brain-melting screen time.

The trick, he was learning, was to get Rylnn out of Maverick's house before she got bored with banging on whatever scrap he'd given her, and turned to something much more interesting, such as decorating a newly redone wall with a marker. Or trying to outfit Dylan with a tiara.

Although that was fun for everyone. And honestly, the guys were awesome about Ry tagging along. They even curbed their swearing around her.

But they weren't dads and didn't always get it, didn't always foresee the oncoming storm brewing on the horizon. Landon still occasionally missed the meltdown signs himself, but was getting better at it.

He hoisted Rylnn into the backseat of his huge SUV with the tinted windows, thinking he probably should have kept his truck. This beast was roughly the same size and got about the same mileage. Darn the parenting guilt that had been coupled with that TV commercial his teammate Mullens had been in. Together, they'd convinced him this was safer for Rylnn. Plus his nanny thought it was "boss" or "it slaps," or some other term that had become slang for "cool" and "awesome."

So now Landon was paying off the fancy ride instead of driving his truck. But what was the point of having money if you didn't use it to solve your problems? Maybe he should push a bit harder on his agent to leverage his image like he had for Mullens—get Landon in some commercials or ads so he had extra financial headroom.

"Dude, you don't even know how I want my coffee," Dylan complained from Maverick's front porch.

"Large. One cream, one sugar. Except Athena has us all on a no-sugar, low-fat diet," he called back, referring to the team's dietician. "So a large with a sad little drop of skim milk."

Dylan scowled, aiming one of his crutches at Landon. "You're a killjoy. You know that?"

"Not willing to break the rules?" Landon smirked, well aware that he was likely to get the man his favorite coffee fixings, because when you were benched, what was an extra shot of cream and a spoonful of sugar? Besides, at this point, indulging in a little comfort wouldn't change the direction their season was heading. The Dragons were a new team with one year under their belt. They were basically a collecting ground for almost-retired players, injured ones like himself and Dylan, and rookies so young they were still wet behind the ears.

"Do I look like Mullens?" Dylan asked.

Landon laughed. The team's forward played the rules fast and loose, and was most willing to break their team dietician's meal plan. Why Athena put up with the guy was beyond Landon.

"I want two cookies," Rylnn announced, as Landon finished buckling her in.

"If Mrs. Fisher has them down at the Longhorn, you can have any kind you want."

"Two!" She raised two fingers.

"A good dad would get you two, wouldn't he?" Dylan said encouragingly.

Landon shot him a look. "When you have kids, I'm going to remember this."

His teammate laughed and started back inside. "You still owe me for the nail polish."

Three weeks ago the nanny had bought Rylnn peel-off nail polish. Landon hadn't had the heart to tell her he felt she was too young for it and had let it slide. Rylnn had somehow convinced Dylan he'd look amazing with sparkly pink nails. Which he had.

The four-year-old had bent the man around her little finger with apparent ease. Whenever photographers appeared after games Dylan was all scowls. But in enters Ry and he broke out in smiles.

Landon chuckled and shook his head. "You're a good kid, Ry. The best."

"Yup!" She grinned at him and kicked her legs.

Landon drove the few miles of gravel to the main road that led into the small town of Sweetheart Creek. In front of the Longhorn Diner, he parked beside a rusted green truck that made him think of home. He'd grown up in the foothills of the Rocky Mountains, close to family, and had always thought he'd play for the Calgary Flames. But hockey had brought him to Texas, of all things.

A great area of the world, but a bit far from the faces and places his heart recognized as familiar.

He helped Rylnn out of the back of the vehicle, swinging her through the air, causing her to squeal. He set her down gently, took her hand and headed to the sidewalk.

She pointed down the street. "Daddy, what's that?"

He followed her finger and squinted. Ambling toward them was a small, grayish-brown animal. An ailing alley cat?

It came closer, then let out a horrible screech and began moving faster.

Landon quickly opened the diner's door, lifted Rylnn inside and closed it behind them, hoping nobody saw the way they'd fled from the small animal.

"That was an armadillo," he said. They didn't have them in Canada, and until today he'd assumed they were cute, harmless and, like any wild animal, happy to avoid humans.

Through the glass they watched the armadillo waddle past.

"It's ugly," Rylnn said.

"And cranky."

Maybe he needed to rethink the whole get-a-yard for Rylnn, and do some in-depth research on scary Texas wildlife.

* * *

"Sounds like you met either Henry Wylder or Bill the armadillo."

Cass bit back a smile as she waited for Landon Jackson to turn around. His shoulders seemed broader than they'd been last May, which had to be a trick of the eye. Either way, the man was built, and he looked like he could lift her over his shoulder without a second thought.

The enormous smile stretching across his face when he saw her made her own break free.

Why was she grinning like a silly fool? She'd met him only once, and he was a famous hockey player. It wasn't like they were friends or had a flirty *thing* going on between them.

Those facts, however, hadn't stopped her from daydreaming about him during the past five months. The man and his fumbling, big-hearted attempt at parenting a young, strong-minded princess had wormed their way into her thoughts.

And now here he was. Smiling at her.

"Cassandra," he said, making her wish she'd put some effort into her appearance before dropping Dusty off at the library's story hour. "Sorry, your friends call you Cass, right?" He gave her a hopeful look.

She laughed, pleased that he remembered. Especially when he must meet so many people. So many women. "Yeah, you can call me Cass. Hey, Rylnn." She took in the dark-skinned girl's wild curls, gorgeous princess dress and plastic jewelry, complete with tiara. Cass's parents would never have indulged her with something so impractical as a princess costume beyond a possible Halloween splurge, but it sure looked fun.

"We just saw an ugly kitty."

"That's an armadillo. We call him Bill." Cass peered through the glass door to confirm they'd been running from him and not the town's curmudgeon, Henry. She felt a bit lightheaded from watching Landon, a hulking athlete, rescue his daughter in her pretty dress.

She'd needed a man like him last week when she'd found a raccoon in the living room, drinking from one of the pots she'd put out to catch rainwater. Well, she supposed she didn't actually need a man, as she'd been able to chase it out of the house on her own. But the idea of having someone like Landon whisk her away from potential danger held an appeal she couldn't explain.

"Do you like my new dress?" Rylnn twirled, showing off the blue Cinderella costume.

"It's very nice."

"Daddy bought it for me."

"He's a good dad."

Landon's grin widened and his shoulders straightened.

His faded sweatshirt was covered with streaks of dust and slivers of old wood, and he smelled like hot metal. Somehow, in spite of his disheveled state, he looked even more handsome than he had at the Mother's Day dance. Was it due to the appealing fact that he must have been working on something, getting his hands dirty, like he was an average Joe and not a pampered sports celebrity?

Carly Clarke, one of Cass's new friends in town, moved past them with a hello. She gave Rylnn a special, secretive smile, her cowboy boots clacking against the diner's floor, her light pink bandanna holding back her curls and bringing out the soft undertones in her dark skin.

"Are there cowgirl princesses?" Rylnn asked, as soon as Carly was out the door.

"There are," Cass said without thinking. "Do you want to be one?"

"I want cookies." Rylnn pivoted toward the counter.

"Go see what Mrs. Fisher has today," Landon called after her. He said to Cass, "This town might actually have the power to break her princess phase. Though I'm not so sure about the wildlife." He gave a wry glance back toward the door.

"Sweetheart Creek is pretty awesome. Thinking of moving?" Another NHL superstar moving to town? Could Cass call dibs? Not that she had the time or energy—or desire—to try her hand at love again.

But still. Hot. Handsome. Rich. As well as an adorable possibly-single dad.

Sign her up for some swooning from afar.

"Ry needs a yard. A place to play and get dirty, you know? I was thinking maybe the suburbs. Get a dog and all that. But maybe I could swing a place out here. It's not crazy-far from the city."

Cass blinked, waiting for him to let on that he was joking. Because a man who wanted the white-picket-fence family dream? If he was for real, he had to have a long line-up of women begging to be his girlfriend—assuming he didn't have two or three already.

"I want Ry to have a normal childhood."

Cass laughed. Normal. Sure. With a famous dad? Good luck. Although, if they lived out here it might actually become somewhat doable.

"Looks like you already found a fixer-upper." She brushed a clump of cobwebs and dust from Landon's shoulder.

He self-consciously ruffled his hair. "Sorry, I've been crawling around under Maverick's sink all morning."

She picked a bit of something out of his

mussed-up locks. "Ah. You're over at the money pit, huh?"

"You know, fresh air, dirt and a taste of real life... Can't beat it." He gave her a sheepish grin that made her heart flip-flop in her chest.

She glanced toward Rylnn, who was at the back of the diner, climbing onto a tall red stool so she could peer through the cookie platter's glass cover. There were several stacks of cookies and Cass wondered if they'd be leaving with at least one of each kind.

"And you're taking Rylnn over there?"

"Quality father-daughter time."

Was he kidding? Sure, he'd seemed new to fatherhood in May, but letting a four-year-old loose in Maverick's demo zone felt a tad reckless.

"We have to balance out Princess Barbie—the nanny," he said with a long sigh. Landon shifted his weight, and she could tell he felt judged for his parenting choices.

"Is the nanny really that bad?"

His shoulders sagged. "She's the best the agency had."

"I'm sure there are plenty of suitable women out there who'd be happy to work for you."

He visibly shuddered.

Right. She'd momentarily forgotten he was

famous. He probably had to be extra stringent about the recruitment process in order to weed out those who wished to be a nanny for the wrong reasons.

"Why do you call her Princess Barbie?"

"Not to her face," he said quickly. "But, uh, because she strengthens the tendency for Ry to act helpless and adore all things girlie."

"And so you're balancing it out by taking her to a construction zone?" Cass struggled to hide her amusement. Men had such a refreshingly simple take on parenting.

"I want her to feel strong, and to know how to fix things on her own. You know? I'm trying to raise her the right way."

"There's a right way?" Cass nearly laughed. The way he was trying so hard was adorable. He was also so unlike Dusty's father.

"I guess there isn't. But I don't want to screw her up. When she wakes up in the mornings, *I* want to be there. Her *family*. Not some paid stranger who encourages the fans waiting on the sidewalk out front. Which is another strike against the suburbs. Less security and protection."

"You do need to move out here. Stuff like that never happens."

Landon ran a hand down his face as though he could rub away the doubts of parenthood, and Cass wanted to give him a hug. She might struggle in her own way, but if she failed, it would at least be relatively private, unlike for Landon. If Rylnn turned into a rebellious, trouble-seeking teen it would be in the papers, with all blame pointed solely at him.

"I want her to grow up competent and capable. Confident," Landon said quietly. "Like that woman who just left."

"Carly."

"Yeah." His eyes met hers. "Or you."

* * *

Cass blinked at Landon. "You want her to be like me?"

She was so serious, so disbelieving, Landon wanted to chuckle. "You made an impression on her."

Him, too, if he was being honest with himself.

"I did?"

"After the Mother's Day dance, one of her Barbies became a cowgirl. You don't know how big that is."

Cass laughed, her face brightening with delight. "I love it."

"Me, too." He wanted to infuse small-town caring and that sense of community and strength into his little girl's heart, teach her she could be her own superhero, or fairy godmother. Whatever she needed, she could take care of it herself. Save the day or make her own wishes come true.

"I doubt that was my influence, though. There were about a hundred cowgirls present at the dance." Cass's hand rested above her bosom, her wild, wavy hair barely tamed by a wide cloth headband. Her flannel shirt hung open over a fitted tee and jeans that were worn in all the right places. She was one hot rancher mama, that was for sure. He'd thought of her many times over the past several months, but she was even more amazing in reality than in his dreams. A little more tired maybe, but just as stunning with that casual, healthy-outdoor-chick look she had going on.

For a moment, he got lost in her gaze, wondering what it would be like to take her out on a date. There was something about her that was so…familiar and easy. Like meeting up with an old friend he'd been missing for decades.

"Where's Rylnn's mom?" she asked.

"I have a nanny."

Cass quirked her head, but didn't press. He didn't want to get into the story of how he'd been a sperm donor for his best friend after her cancer went into remission. Zofia had wanted to be a mom more than anything and things were looking good. However, her journey had ended a lot sooner than anyone had ever expected, and he knew Rylnn missed her terribly. So did he.

"Princess Barbie," Cass confirmed. "But it sounds like she's not the right fit for your family?"

"Exactly!" It felt surprisingly reassuring hearing someone else say it. "But maybe I'm too fussy," he murmured, testing his mom's theory on Cass.

"No such thing when it's your kid," she said immediately. She shifted forward, squeezing his arm with a look of sympathy. She smelled like peppermint, making him think of Christmas and cold winter nights in the foothills, snow falling peacefully outside the window.

"Yeah?"

She nodded, her conviction reassuring. "If you're ever in a bind..." She laughed and backed away, taking the scented memories with her. "Oh, you hardly even know me. See where flattery gets you?" She waved a hand, looking almost embarrassed. "You end up with strangers offering to babysit for you."

"Would you? Babysit?" He felt himself leaning in, waiting for an answer. To him, she didn't feel like a stranger. She felt familiar, almost as if she'd always been in his circle and was someone he could rely on. Someone who understood his values because they were hers, too.

That made no sense. But his gut was telling him this was it, and long ago he'd learned to listen when it spoke about something important.

Cass shrugged, her cheeks pink, her gaze everywhere but on him. Then, slowly, she allowed her eyes to drift his way, to crawl up his torso and meet his gaze. "I mean, sure. Yes. If you're comfortable with that. I live at least an hour away from you, though."

He nodded quickly, understanding it was a long shot, but even so, a weight lifted off his shoulders.

"Yeah, no. Of course," he said, running a hand through his hair and dislodging more dust. "Thank you. I appreciate it."

"It's nice to know—as a parent, and a single parent especially—that there's a backup plan, even though you'll probably never use it."

"Exactly." Their eyes met again, and a shot of warmth wove its way through his core. "I should get your number in case." Landon raised his brows in what he hoped was an innocent and charming way.

Cass laughed, her hand coming up to the neck of her tee. She toyed with the thin chain of her necklace, then reached out to put her number in his phone.

He texted her a smiley face. "Now you have mine, too."

She pulled out her phone to check her the messages. "I'm going to sell that to some swooning fans for big bucks, you know."

Please, no. He'd already had to change his number twice in the last year.

"I'm kidding! Don't look so stricken." She laughed, apparently amused by his distress.

"Well, just so you know," he said, trying for humor as he cleared his throat, "when they're out front of my condominium screaming for The Blockade, that's me." His smile felt pained.

"What?" Her amusement faded.

"My nickname on the ice. I'm the goalie." She stared blankly at him and he felt like a fool. She wasn't the type to swoon. At least not for a hockey star, and here he was throwing his fame around like it somehow made him more worthy of her attention.

"You're serious? They really do go that far?"

He gave a quick nod, and noted how her worried glance darted toward Rylnn, making him feel as though his own anxieties about his daughter and her sense of normalcy and safety weren't completely unfounded.

He cleared his throat again. "Cool. Well, you know, if you need someone to talk trucks with Dusty..." He glanced around in case he'd missed spotting the boy earlier.

"Oh, don't tempt me!" Cass smiled, the worried expression gone. She bit her lower lip in a very encouraging way. It made him want to nibble on it himself. "He never stops talking about them."

"We can get together and make a trade—princess talk for truck talk."

He gestured toward Rylnn, who was asking Mrs. Fisher to package up cookies. The waitress gave him a questioning look as she held up tongs and an empty bag. He nodded.

"Not so up-to-date on my princesses," Cass admitted.

"Do you like tea parties?" he asked, aware he was actually flirting.

No women during the season.

Like he'd have time for a woman right now, anyway.

"Love 'em."

He wasn't sure if she was serious or not.

"Uh. Hey, can I ask what do you do for child care?" Landon rested a hand against the diner's doorframe. "It's just you, right?"

She nodded. "Dusty's in the library program at the moment, but I call on my sister—she lives next door—to babysit sometimes."

"You moved here from Montana, right? Recently?"

"Yeah."

"Rancher?"

"I was, but Alexa and I sold it all last spring."

"And now you have…what was it? A hunting lodge?" Landon eyed her boots, then her tanned nose dotted with freckles. She looked like a cowgirl through and through, not a hunter. She also looked pleased that he had remembered bits about her. Like he could have forgotten. Rylnn wasn't the only one she'd made an impression on at the dance.

"Yeah. It's on a few dozen acres. I'm going to turn it into an event center. But I need to make some more money so I can afford to fix it up all the way." He could see the weariness of single-parenthood and entrepreneurship weighing on her, no doubt responsible for the smudges of fatigue under her eyes.

"Basically, I need a job where I can get paid to work on the lodge while being a stay-at-home mom." She glanced at her watch. "Oh, I gotta run before Karen—the librarian—thinks I've abandoned Dusty. Great to see you." She flashed him a smile that hit him in the solar plexus, radiating warmth through his core.

As Cass headed onto the street, she left Landon with a brilliant idea he wasn't so sure she'd go for.

CHAPTER 3

"*H*ello?" Cass held her phone closer to her ear and frowned. Surely her eyes had deceived her when she'd read the caller ID. Landon Jackson was phoning her already? They'd been together at the Longhorn only an hour and a half ago.

She could hear road noise through the line and wondered if he'd accidentally dialed her.

"Hello?"

"Hey, Cass. Long time no see," Landon said easily, his deep voice warm and wonderful.

Not an accidental dial. He'd called her on purpose.

She closed the fridge and looked for a place to sit down.

Wait. Was he calling her to babysit for him? Already? Had she walked into a trap laid by a charmer who used his fame to pave the way to get what he wanted?

That didn't seem like him, but her instincts had failed her in the past.

Cass put Landon on Speaker and set her phone on the kitchen counter, furiously summoning up reasonable-sounding excuses to say no. Because seriously. Did he have no planning skills? What had she been thinking, making that offer? She'd been dazzled by the way he looked at her, as though he actually saw her—and liked what he saw even though she'd been wearing grubby old jeans and layered shirts that probably smelled of dust and desperation.

In ranching country, a woman didn't have to put in a ton of effort for a man to notice her. Simply back up a pickup truck with a trailer in one quick move and you'd earn enough respect that he'd take you in like a long drink of ice-cold sweet tea on a hot Texas day.

She knew that. She shouldn't be swayed so easily by a sweet smile and a little attention. Especially since Landon carried himself like a man raised on a ranch. He knew the rules.

And yet the way he made her feel was different. It was as if he'd sucked out all the water from her internal well and left her wanting the quenching refill that only he seemed able to provide.

"What's up?" she asked, opening the fridge again so she could transfer leftovers onto the counter. Would this mishmash make a casserole if she added a can of mushroom soup?

"Just heading back to the city," Landon said. "Ry's asleep and so I got to thinking."

"Okay." She was getting curious now. Had she missed the memo where they called and chatted like they were old friends?

She might not actually mind that, but currently she was waiting for the other shoe to drop. Why was he phoning her?

"I was thinking about our conversation in the Longhorn."

She sighed. Yep. Babysitting.

"It seems like we both have problems," he continued.

That was putting it mildly.

"I think you have more than I do," she said.

That wasn't true, but the last thing she needed was to complain about her growing issues, from Dusty's health to her dwindling bank account, with an NHL player. When she'd sold the family ranch in Montana, half had gone to Alexa and half to her. She now owned the Peppermint Lodge free and clear, and had a lump sum for them to live off of, as well as do enough renovations to get the place running as a wedding venue. Sort of.

She hadn't counted on the possibility of looming, massive medical bills as Dusty's doctors' appointments mounted, along with more and more tests as they tried to dig their way to the bottom of what was going on.

She also hadn't counted on crashing her truck. Thank goodness for the loan of Alexa's old one, because here she was.

"Child care and money," Landon said confidently, like he was pitching a business to investors. "We both need child care so we can make money, right?"

She closed the fridge and took him off Speaker, putting the phone to her ear again. She glanced out the kitchen window to make sure Dusty was still outside playing with the kittens that had been born under the back porch.

"Geography is a bit of an issue, but what about this?" Landon proposed.

"Are you still there?" she asked, when he didn't continue. She checked her phone. Still connected.

"I'm probably putting my nose where it absolutely doesn't belong." His tone was apologetic and Cass froze, not daring to breathe. Living in a small town, she was used to people knowing her problems, but Landon Jackson? She wanted him to think of her as that capable and amazing woman who made his daughter want to play with a cowgirl Barbie. She wanted him to keep looking at her as though she were someone whole and incredible.

Not a struggling someone with problems she might not be able to handle.

And his tone hinted that he knew the truth about her. She had problems she possibly couldn't handle.

"Tell me," she demanded.

"Mav says you've got medical bills accumulating, and that something's up with Dusty."

She shook her head. Small towns. Absolutely nothing was private. Nothing.

"Yup." She blinked and inhaled, trying to quell the panic inside. Her basic medical insurance plan was soon to be outpaced by Dusty's needs. And if the doctor's hunch was right and Dusty had something going on with his heart…

She blinked back tears, pressing her lips together.

"What if..." Landon hesitated.

"Spit it out. Rip off the Band-Aid."

"What if I paid those bills and moved to Sweetheart Creek with Rylnn?"

"What!"

She didn't know where the man was coming from. Whatever he was proposing, he had balls, that was for certain.

"I'd keep my condo in the city, but we'd make Sweetheart Creek our home, and you'd help me care for Rylnn."

"Like a nanny?"

Because that's what she needed to solve her problems—another kid in her care. Dusty had just started kindergarten and now she had six hours of free time most weekdays to take care of business. Taking on Rylnn would eat up those free hours.

"Yeah." The hope in his voice had her shaking her head.

"You can find one in San Antonio," she said firmly. "Qualified, vetted, experienced ones who, when they sing in a forest, have birds come and perch on their outstretched hand."

She heard something that sounded like Landon holding in a laugh. Darn it, but that made her almost forgive his boldness.

"Not really what I'm looking for," he said, amusement in his tone. "I'm hoping for someone real. Kind but tough. Like you."

She sucked in a deep breath and held it for several seconds so she wouldn't cave to his flattery. It had been a long time since a man had thought her personality was worth praising.

A woman like her.

His earlier words still felt good when they surfaced in her memory. And that was surely dangerous.

No. It wouldn't work. What was she thinking? She'd get derailed from what she really wanted to accomplish if she became his daughter's nanny. She'd put herself second for too long, and that stopped now. Dusty could come first, but not some guy in need of child care.

She wanted to turn her lodge into a wedding venue by summer. Next winter at the latest.

She hadn't asked Archer for child support in eons because it was uncomfortable having that conversation, even when she could have used the cash. Plus she'd been afraid that if she started asking for money he might insist she stay in the same state as him, or even demand the odd visit. She'd even kept running the Montana ranch for several years after her heart was no longer in it because she didn't want to tell Alexa she wanted to sell their childhood home.

But she'd call Archer for medical bill assistance before she'd indebt herself to Landon.

"I can't help you. I have things to do."

"Please think about it."

"Landon, even if I wanted to, I have—"

"I'm not looking for full-time. I mean, not in the nine-to-five sense. It's a lot of hours, but the kids could play together when Dusty's not at kindergarten, which hopefully would be less of a burden on you so you could do your stuff around the lodge. I'm around a few mornings each week, and then in the evenings, when I'm at games, you could probably squeeze in more stuff while the kids play."

"I'm not a nanny."

"I know. She needs family, Cass."

"I'm not family."

"You and Dusty, and that town and a yard—it would do a lot more for her than a nanny who's been hired to dote on her like a lady-in-waiting. Rylnn means everything to me and I really don't want to screw her up. I want to give her a life that grounds her."

"Why me? You could hire—"

"Snow White? No, thanks."

"A real nanny."

"You've made an impression on her."

"She barely knows me."

"She talks about you. She doesn't talk about the nanny."

"Flattery won't work on me, Landon."

"It's not flattery. It's the truth. You have the right personality to bring out the best in her."

"I have things to do while Dusty is at school. And I'm not into dresses."

"I know." There was warmth in his voice she couldn't ignore. "I want someone who's going to let her be big and loud and brave. I want her to have a cheerleader in her life, a strong adult female who won't crush her beautiful, crazy spirit."

Cass bit the inside of her cheek. Every little girl deserved a dad like him. A dad who'd ask for the impossible just in case there was a sliver of a chance he'd get it.

"I know it's a nutso idea, Cass."

"It is."

"But I'd cover your medical bills. Add in a wage, too."

Okay, now he was just talking crazy, because that was a lot of money. And if she accepted, then she'd end up being a nanny, at his beck and call, until the kid was married off. Plus, she'd forget all about her own projects.

She needed to think about this, though. No medical bills would mean she could funnel more finances toward getting the lodge ready so it could earn an income stream for them sooner rather than later. No shortcuts or compromises like with her current plan.

And the kids *could* play together after school, freeing up some of her time. She'd also gotten quite a bit done around the place with Dusty underfoot. Surely she could do the same with Rylnn around?

She was looking at possibly fewer hours to work on the lodge, but more money to spend on getting things done.

But Landon would really move farther from work so his daughter could have what he felt was good for her? He didn't even know Cass. Who was to say that she'd actually be good for Rylnn? Surely someone else could step in for the girl.

What if Cass counted on him and his money, and then things got tough and he said sayonara?

"We both need help." The vulnerability in Landon's voice almost made her agree to the idea. It took a lot of courage—or desperation—to ask this of her. But she also understood being willing to do anything for your kid.

"I need someone like you, Cass. Please, will you consider it?"

* * *

"Cass?" Landon said in surprise when he'd opened his condo door. He stepped aside to allow her to come in, but she didn't move.

He didn't have to check his watch to know it was well after ten or eleven at night, since Rylnn had been in bed for several hours already.

The last time he'd spoken to Cassandra Mc-Tavish was over a week ago, when he'd made his nanny proposal.

"How do you know where I live?" he demanded, realizing that was the least important thing he could ask. And yet it was intriguing. His building had a doorman to keep fans from pounding on his front door or harassing his neighbors. How did Cass get past him? She wasn't on the list and nobody had buzzed up.

With her hands deep in her jacket pockets, she tipped forward and back in her cowboy boots. "I thought about your idea."

"Come in," Landon suggested.

She shook her head.

"So? What do you think?" he asked.

Cass inhaled, then finally stepped past him, entering the condo. Seconds later she halted, eyes wide as she gazed around his professionally decorated living space. His housekeeper kept his wood floors shiny and the place dust free. The fingerprints and endless crumbs from having a four-year-old, however, were a little harder to stay on top of during the housekeeper's five hours a week.

"Come in, come in," Landon said, moving past Cass in the wide hall. Being Canadian, he had a thing for removing outside footwear, but it was clear Cass wasn't in a state to deal with his inborn habits. He hurried into the living room with its view of San Antonio's brightly lit downtown. "I was just folding laundry."

He grabbed the pile of wrinkled clothing off the couch and snatched the remote, muting the sports highlights. He hated to miss them, especially when there was a chance they might feature him blocking shots. He had stopped a lot of pucks tonight, but he'd also let more through than the other team's goalie, meaning they'd lost the game.

Again. The team was having a rough season

and his teammates were complaining about the lack of commercial offers and the like.

He tried not to get sucked into it, but he'd dearly love to grow the distance between his assets and liabilities, putting the former firmly in the lead.

"I can't stay," Cass said, stopping at the end of the hall.

She was pale, her brow furrowed with worry.

"Are you okay? Where's Dusty?" Landon dropped the laundry back onto the couch, then balled two small pink socks together before tossing them across the room into an empty laundry basket. Two points.

He glanced at Cass, but she hadn't seemed to notice his athletic prowess.

"I was thinking about your deal, and I would like to propose something different."

Landon perched on the back of the couch, facing her.

"I want to sell live Christmas trees, and I'm hoping you'll be a silent partner. I need seed money and the banks are too slow."

"You're going to grow trees?"

She shook her head, the wisps of hair that had fallen out of her brown braid dancing across her cheeks. "No, fully grown, ready to sell. I don't have enough upfront to put in an order on my own. Here's the pitch, including projected sales and profits." She handed him a folded printout from her pocket. "My overhead fees are low, but the trees will cost a lot. Profits will be decent and I've proposed your cut." She gestured to the page.

"What were you thinking?" Landon asked, dropping the paper on the couch cushions behind him. The way she looked tonight, tired and worried, he didn't want a dime of her money.

"Fifty-fifty. And five percent interest on the loan."

"No interest, and five percent of the profits," he countered.

"That's too little."

"And you're offering up too much." He reached for the paper, glanced at it, then tossed it back on the couch. "You'll start selling trees next month and be done within several weeks. It's a small, temporary loan. Really, no interest needed. Where's Dusty?"

"How about 40 percent of the profits?" She wouldn't look at him, her hands bunching.

"Cass?" He moved across the floor, his concern growing.

"He's at the children's hospital overnight. Having tests."

"Tests?"

"He got really dizzy at school. There's something wrong with his heart."

Landon's breath left him. "Cass," he whispered. He wanted to tug her into his arms, but feared she would refuse him, and that a hug might breach the wall of strength she'd built in order to get through her day.

"Counter offer?"

Her bottom lip trembled, and mentally, he said, *"Screw it."* He pulled her in, holding her tight in the warmest hug he could give. "What do you need? What can I do, Cass?"

Her body shook, but she didn't let out the sob that was surely trying to break free.

He couldn't imagine what she must be feeling right now.

She pushed him away and swiped at her eyes. "Forty percent of the profits?"

"I'll front the money. Pay me back whenever you've earned it. And whatever this current visit to the hospital costs, I'll cover it."

"No."

"I will. But next week, if it's not too much with what's going on with Dusty, I'll drop Rylnn off at your place as a test. One week of babysitting."

"But don't you have a nanny?"

"She's been asking for time off to go visit her family."

Cass sniffed, nodding.

Was that a yes?

As Landon watched her, he could practically see the weight lift from her shoulders.

"Partners?" he asked, holding out his hand.

"Forty percent of the profits."

"Not a chance. Loan payback within three months without interest, and take Rylnn for five days as a test. If it's not working, we can pull the plug sooner."

Cass hesitated, staring at his still-extended hand. Then she put her palm in his and gave it a shake. "Okay. But I'm covering Dusty's bill."

"I'm offering."

"I have the money, and he comes before the lodge reno or anything else."

"Okay. But know that if Dusty ever needs a guy to step in for a Father's Day event or to talk trucks or something, you can call on me." He tried for a smile to lighten things, to let her know that, if he could, he'd be there beyond just his wallet. He wasn't some jerk taking advantage of a mom who was having troubles.

She glanced at him sideways, eyes narrowed.

Maybe he'd pushed it a bit far.

"Or if you need a plus one, I can also help you out." He tried for a dazzling grin.

Now she was practically rolling her eyes, but at least she was smiling. "Landon…"

"What?"

Her cheeks were pink, and she seemed slightly flustered. "What are you playing at?"

"House."

"You're trying to play house? With me?" Her mouth twisted as if she was holding in a laugh.

"Sure. Why not? We can help each other out, right? Two single parents, leaning on each other."

She let go of the laugh, filling the room with it. "You're incredibly overconfident."

He shrugged and grinned again.

"Taking advantage of a woman who's having a tough go… Not what I expected, Landon Jackson!" Her hands were on her hips and she had a glare in her eyes, but he could tell she didn't truly mean it. She was trying to cover up the way he'd made her heart beat a little faster. The way he'd made her skin flush.

Or at least that's what he'd like to believe.

He waited for her to say more, but she didn't, just wordlessly turned down the hallway to the door.

"I'm not a bad guy, Cass," he said, following her. "Ask Mav."

He winced. His friend Maverick didn't exactly have the best reputation at the moment, so maybe didn't make the best character reference.

She closed the door behind her, cutting off his view of her curvaceous outline and her shaking head.

*   *   *

"Hot date?"

Cass, who had been digging around in her shoulder bag for her wallet, looked up at Jenny Oliver. "What?"

Jenny shrugged as she wrapped up the pink lace bra. "I don't know. You seem lost in thought. Could be nervous about the man who's going to see you in this after your hot date." She pushed the tissue-wrapped undergarment across the counter.

"I wish." Cass handed over her credit card and dropped the package from the sale bin into her bag. She'd come into Blue Tumbleweed on a whim, not realizing her friend sold all layers of Western wear from top to bottom. "Dusty was wearing my bra as a kitten carrier."

Jenny giggled. "That's cute."

It had been. He'd been walking around the yard with a kitten in each cup. Sadly, the bra had been pretty much clawed to bits by the time she'd gotten it back from him a day and a half later.

"He needs a male role model," she confided. "He should be using my bras as slingshots, not baby slings."

"Is he feeling better, then?"

"Not really. That was the perkiest he's been all week."

"Poor kid." Jenny handed back Cass's card. "Well, maybe your pretty new undergarments will bring you a man. You know, if you wear it, he will come."

Both women giggled. "That's the dream."

"Although…not *too* soon," April Wylder, Jenny's shop assistant, called from where she was sorting blouses on a sale rack.

They burst into another round of giggles.

"Not that Brant—"

"We don't want to hear about you and your husband!" Jenny exclaimed, startling Cass.

April shrugged, unbothered, and went back to sorting clothing. Jenny lowered her voice so only Cass could hear. "She's expecting, and her pregnancy hormones…" Jenny rolled her eyes and gave a dramatic shudder.

"At least I'm getting some," April called.

"Does being pregnant make your hearing better? Seriously, April."

The woman chuckled.

Cass shifted her weight. "There's sort of a guy…"

"Really?" Jenny perked up.

"No, not like that," Cass said quickly. "He's asked me to be his nanny."

Jenny's whole body drooped as though somebody had let the air out of her full-figured build. "You're kidding me. So no tender kisses in the crook of your elbow, where the skin is supersensitive and it makes you shiver?" Her expression grew dreamy.

"'The crook of your elbow'?" Cass repeated. Not sexy. Not even close. "Your love life is sadder than I realized."

"What? It's sensual!"

"Uh, no."

"Then where?"

Cass shrugged. "Depends on the kisser. My sister, Alexa, swears by neck kisses. Me? Behind the knee."

Jenny leaned closer. "Really?"

"Totally."

Jenny considered it. "Nah. Those spots are meh. This tender skin here—" she tapped the inner crease of her elbow "—total erogenous zone."

"I'll take that into account."

Not that anyone would be kissing her anytime soon.

She turned to go, but Jenny stopped her by reaching across the counter and taking her arm. "So? Who asked you to be his nanny? Are you going to do it?"

Seeing that April was peering over the rack at them again, the two women huddled closer. "Landon Jackson."

She waited as Jenny's face scrunched, then brightened as she placed the name. "The NHL player!"

"Shh!"

"The Blockade? The goalie? For the Dragons? He's hot."

"I know."

"But he asked you to be his nanny?" Jenny's nose scrunched again.

"I'm so over looking for love. Tried it. Didn't work out. Time to make other people's dreams come true with a wedding event center."

Jenny eyed her. "You haven't given up on love. You still believe. You still enjoy the odd fantasy about true love finding you when you're not paying any attention."

"I will deny that all day long."

"We're good at lying to ourselves. So? The nanny thing?"

"He offered to pay for Dusty's last hospital stay."

Jenny's eyes widened. "No. What did you say?"

"I said no!"

"No?"

"The last thing I need is another kid to look after, or to be indebted to some rich guy. I have a rickety old lodge to transform into a beautiful wedding venue."

Jenny shook her head, pressing a hand against Cass's. "No, the last thing you need are big medical bills. Your kid's going to be in college before you know it. You don't want to be still paying off bills from this decade." She propped a fist under her chin and leaned on the counter. "How long would you be indebted to him?"

"I don't know."

"You don't know?"

"I didn't say yes." Cass sighed. "Well, I said yes to babysitting his daughter for a week."

"A week!"

"A week for what?" April called.

"Nothing." She lowered her voice. "Actually, five days."

"Five days in exchange for paying those bills? *Five?*"

Cass winced. It was an unreasonable exchange, one that weighed heavily in her favor. "I said no. I went to him for tree money."

"So you have tree money and a babysitting gig? But said no to being a nanny and having your bills paid off?"

"It just felt like he was…"

"Buying you. Overcompensating for something? Hinting that his daughter is actually a demon child? Get over it. Take advantage of his desperation."

"Yeah, but…"

"Too good to be true?"

Cass nodded.

"Wondering where the catch is?"

She nodded again.

Jenny straightened. "Put your pride on the shelf. This guy is like a guardian angel with a giant bank account, coming down to save you. You're living in a movie—a romantic comedy."

Cass gave her a chiding look.

"Okay, I know. Guilty pleasure. Don't tell anyone. I'm still a big baddy with a tough heart you can't break."

She studied her friend, wondering if people saw her as capable as Jenny. Secretly, the two of them seemed to have the same fears and dreams. Pretty standard stuff, actually. The fear that she wasn't enough. That she couldn't do it all, and that ridiculous heaps of help would actually be really nice, but she'd never have the courage to ask for it. Or accept.

"This is where you agree that I'm tough, Cass."

"Yes! Of course you are. Toughest of the tough!"

Jenny rolled her eyes.

"Should I have agreed to his proposal?" Cass asked.

"I think so." Her friend's eyes danced. "Maybe if you're a good nanny you'll get one of those sensual kisses." She tapped the inside of her arm.

"That's not the sexiest place to get kissed. I'm just saying."

"Yeah, you're thinking about him kissing you behind the knees, aren't you?" Jenny called with a laugh as Cass exited the store.

Yeah.

It was true. She was.

That and Landon trailing kisses along her collarbone, and how good it would feel to lose herself in someone else's touch for just a few minutes.

* * *

I'll take care of it.

Could there be five sexier words in the human language?

That's what Landon had said when, after her five days of babysitting, she'd agreed to be his nanny if he paid for Dusty's last stay in the hospital.

He hadn't even blinked at the tally at the bottom of the invoice.

He'd simply folded the sheet in half, met her gaze with something akin to calm determination and said, "I'll take care of it."

Swoon.

Jenny was right.

Cass was living in some sort of dream or movie where the heroine was blessed with a magical man who'd swept down from the heavens with a bank account that fixed everything.

And Landon had been right, too. Taking care of two kids—when Dusty wasn't in school—was almost easier in some ways. Despite having a silver spoon at her disposal, Rylnn wasn't that different from Dusty. She was happy with mac 'n' cheese for lunch, got cranky when tired, loved story time at the library and could spend hours carting kittens around in one of Cassie's old bras. Yes, she'd lost another brassiere to the outdoors, but at least it wasn't her pretty new one.

And Dusty loved having a playmate and seemed dazzled by her energy. The girl was a ray of sunshine, full of life.

Landon, however, was looking more and more beat. He was schlepping back and forth from the city, spending hours on the road without complaint, the fatigue in his eyes growing deeper each day.

The fact that he was willing to make such a sacrifice, one that surely impacted his work, pulled at her. He could step beyond his pride and accept help himself.

And apparently she could accept way too much financial help in return for giving him that assistance.

She needed to be careful, though. Big promises made by a man in need were a surefire way to disappoint. She'd learned that lesson before.

Although…a zero balance when it came to her medical debts… That alone had her weeping silently in the kitchen for a solid three minutes before she'd pulled herself together, reminding herself there would be many more bills to come. But Cass felt much more capable of handling the future knowing she was moving forward from zero rather than from in the red.

Feeling a bubble of happiness rise within her given the way things were working out, she pulled over a few parking spots down from the Longhorn Diner, put the truck in Park and turned to face the kids in the backseat. They'd just come from story time with Karen at the library, where they'd cuddled the library dog, Ribbons, while listening to her read. They'd both been silent the last few blocks, absorbed in their haul of borrowed picture books.

"Who wants a cookie?" Cass asked.

"Me!" Rylnn called.

"Me, too!" Dusty agreed.

"Excellent. So do I." Cass got out, collected the kids and ushered them to the sidewalk.

"A is for armadillo!" Rylnn announced, pointing down the sidewalk as they crossed to the diner's door. A round gray creature, about the size of a cat, was ambling toward them.

"That's Bill," Dusty said, backing up.

"No, I don't think so," Cass said, watching the animal waddle. "This one seems…cuter."

Her son turned and headed back to the truck.

"Where are you going?" she asked. "Don't you want a cookie?"

"It's Bill." He climbed into the front passenger-side seat and closed the door.

Cass turned back to the approaching animal. "It's kind of cute in an ugly sort of way, isn't it?"

Rylnn was leaning forward, the October breeze toying with the hem of her pink-and-white princess dress. "It's *so* cute!"

The armadillo bared its teeth and hissed.

Cass and Rylnn both jumped. Cass hoisted the startled girl into her arms, deposited her in the truck, then ran around to the driver's side and climbed in, slamming the door behind her.

"I told you it was Bill," Dusty said calmly.

Cass waited for her heart to stop hammering. "Why on earth did they put that evil little beast on the town's Welcome sign?"

Everyone seemed to hate the critter, but he was grudgingly celebrated as an adored mascot. There was even a drink named after him at the Watering Hole, and talk about holding some sort of fair called Armadillo Day just after New Year's.

They watched as the animal continued down the sidewalk, the kids standing and watching through the windshield, short enough that they didn't knock their heads on the cab's roof.

When the armadillo was far enough away to feel safe, Cass ushered the kids across the sidewalk again.

Brant Wylder, the town veterinarian and animal control officer, met them at the diner door, holding it for them.

"Hey, y'all. Bill got you on the run?" He grinned and tipped his hat at the three of them.

Cass rolled her eyes.

"Cassie wonders why they put him on the Welcome signs," Rylnn said.

Brant shrugged. "Dunno. Hey, do you have a dog?"

Cass shook her head.

"Would you like one?"

"Yeah!" both kids screamed, causing faces to turn and smile at their enthusiasm.

There was definitely no lying low with these kids in tow.

"I've got a Great Dane," Brant said. "He's wonderful with kids—we've been fostering him at our place. But April says between him and the puppy and the upcoming baby, she needs to reclaim some sanity."

"A Great Dane?" It likely weighed well over a hundred pounds, with its head coming up somewhere around Cass's ribs. Those things were like a small horse. And the kids would probably try to ride it like one, too. "I don't know if I can feed a dog that big."

"I'll feed it," Dusty said.

"You can both go pick out a cookie," Cass suggested to the kids. "One. Just one each." She gave Rylnn a pointed look and received a pout in return.

"Do you think Alexa might consider fostering Stockdale until I can find him a permanent home?" Brant asked, the kids hanging on his every word. "The shelter would pay his food and any expenses."

Brant and April were currently running the animal shelter out of Brant's veterinarian office, Call of the Wyld(er), while they secured funding for a building of its own.

"We can take him," Dusty stated.

"Can I name him?" Rylnn asked, tugging on Brant's checkered sleeve.

"He already has a name. It's Stockdale," the vet repeated.

"That's a bad name. It should be Prince Charming," Rylnn argued with a frown.

"He was found on Stockdale Road, so his name is Stockdale."

"That's not a name."

Cass bit back a smile. If she had to place odds on a winner in this conversation, it would be Rylnn. Cass was already learning to pick her battles with the girl, and the girl was learning when Cass's no was a firm one.

"Tell you what," Brant said, adjusting his cowboy hat, his conciliatory tone worrisome, "if Cass agrees to foster Stockdale, you can call him Prince Charming."

Rylnn bounced, her dress flouncing and glittering. "Can we bring him home now?"

"I need to think about this," Cass said slowly. She'd love to have a dog, but would it be too much? And fostering a dog was risky. If the kids became attached, they'd be crushed when he found a forever home.

But adopting a dog Stockdale's size? She'd be agreeing to serve as a nanny for whole new financial reasons.

She didn't mind the idea of Rylnn and Landon sticking around a lot longer.

And that alone should cause her to panic.

But it didn't. And that fact caused her to panic.
Just a little bit.

CHAPTER 4

"They're watching a movie?" Cass asked Landon as he fell into the wicker chair beside her on the porch.

Her foster dog, Prince Charming, looked up at him, but didn't lift his chin from the sun-bleached planking. He gave one tail tap hello. Landon reached out with a foot and rubbed the dog's stomach, wishing his lifestyle would allow him to have a dog of his own.

"Yup. Sounds like they had another good day."

She gave a hum of acknowledgment as he set a container of celery, cucumber and carrot sticks on the table beside him. It was a snack bin he'd asked to leave in her fridge in an effort to stay on track with the team dietician's directives and to meet Athena Gavras' strict daily veggie quota.

Cass peeked at the container. "I told you not to put it at the back of the fridge. Anything against the rear wall freezes."

Landon opened the frost-lined lid and took a bite of frozen celery. He made a face and offered it to the dog, who politely set it on the porch floor after taking a test bite.

This woman needed a new fridge. A new truck, too.

"What did parents do before television?" Landon asked, stretching out his legs.

Dusty had been talking his ear off about his day and the giant spider he'd seen, Rylnn speaking over him about whatever came to mind. To preserve his sanity—and to steal a little time with Cass—he'd suggested a movie.

Rylnn, with a streak of dried mud on her princess dress, was off like a puck shot from an all-star forward, already manning the remote, choosing the movie before Dusty even got into the living room.

Things were good here. Their trial period had ended a few days ago, and they'd agreed to carry on, Landon paying Cass for her nanny time. Over the past week they'd fallen into a new pattern, where on non-game nights Landon would pick up Rylnn after supper, and he and Cass would sit and chat on the porch before he made the drive back to the city. She'd insisted he needed the break, but secretly he believed she enjoyed the adult company after spending all day with the kids.

Personally, he looked forward to his non-game days more than ever. It was relaxing—more relaxing than Coach Louis's meditative sound bath mixes—to sit here, listening to the cattle call to each other over at Alexa's nearby ranch, the birds chirping as the sun went down, the crickets and frogs starting up. That was a sound bath he could get behind.

A few kittens skittered across the wood slats, batting at each other's legs before tumbling off the edge of the porch and into the flowerbed and patch of peppermint growing below.

This place reminded him of home and his own childhood. When he was here, he was just some guy who played high-level hockey for a living. There was no need to be on the lookout for fans ready to ambush him outside his car, no need for tinted windows to give Rylnn privacy.

Peace. Normalcy.

He loved that he'd found a way to provide his daughter a taste of this.

But the drive *was* killing him. The extra hours tacked onto his days were proving to be more than he could comfortably handle.

He sighed and rubbed his face, legs splayed out in front of him as he sagged in the chair.

"Tired?"

"Yeah."

But Rylnn was happy, and he found he could concentrate better in his games and practices—bringing them closer to a win—knowing that his daughter was safe and having a blast in the country.

Maybe part of the magic was that Cass was a mom and so instinctively knew when to push a kid and when to soften. Whatever her magic was, she was the right fit, like his gut had suggested.

But he was having no luck finding a place in town for them to stay so Rylnn could be spared the commute.

Cass was frowning out at the yard and Landon had a feeling she was thinking of all the things she wanted to do to turn the lodge into a wedding venue. He'd seen some of her sketches, and if she brought them to life, her place was going to be amazing.

Either that or she was wondering why there was a black bra hanging on a fence post.

Not his business.

She might have a love life that involved her getting naked in her own yard.

He shook his head. A cowgirl divorcée who obviously had been burned in love was opening her own wedding event center, and throwing her undergarments around outdoors? Cass definitely kept him on his toes.

But the wedding center—did that mean she wasn't bitter and jaded about love? That she truly believed she might find it again? Or was she simply generous of spirit, wanting to help build the hopes and dreams of others?

"Why's your bra out there?"

"Who says it's mine?"

Because he could imagine it on her. Pressing, supporting.

He rubbed his hand down his face and blinked a few times, trying to clear his thoughts. She was his daughter's nanny. She'd given him absolutely no signs she wanted anything but his cold, hard cash.

Landon reached for the mug of peppermint tea Cass had poured for him and lifted it to his lips. The scent cleared his sinuses, and he took a welcome sip of the crisp flavor.

"New brand?" he asked.

"I forgot about it. Steeped it too long."

"I like it."

"It's strong."

"Mmm. Still nice." He could sit here with her, talking or not talking, all night. Around her, he didn't have to be anyone but himself.

He had a feeling it was the same for her, too. There was no show to put on, no fretting about the tea being perfectly brewed. She was dusty from head to foot, no doubt from fixing something, and content to just sit.

The barn cat came up, stepping over the half-comatose dog, and wound herself between Landon's legs, rubbing her head on his calves. He scooped up the mama cat, cuddling her against his chest, where she curled up with a smile and a loud purr. Like the kittens, she smelled of peppermint from walking through the various wild patches that grew on the property.

Landon absorbed himself in the moment and smiled. A cat on his chest, happy kids, sounds of nature around him, and the reassuring presence of a woman at his side.

This moment felt a lot like family.

He smiled and snuggled further into the chair, hoping Cass would let him stay here forever.

* * *

Just ask him.

She was so nervous.

But the bags of fatigue beneath Landon's eyes were growing along with her concern. The man needed someone to cut him a break. Not his kid. *Him.*

She inhaled slowly to steady herself, then broke the stillness of the autumn night. "I have an idea."

"What's that?" Landon was rubbing the cat's ears, her purring loud, her expression one of bliss. "This cat's purr is the best. I can feel it all the way through to my spine."

"Cool," Cass said absently. "I was thinking since you haven't found anywhere close by yet, and because we have lots of room, why don't y'all crash here for a bit? You know, when you're not in the city for your days off."

"Won't that cramp your style?"

His focus had laser-beamed its way to her, and she shifted in her seat, making the wicker chair creak. "What style?" She dusted off her jeans with a laugh.

He gestured toward the black bra hanging on a post, where Dusty had abandoned it after the kittens had grown tired of the carrying game.

Her whole body heated with embarrassment and she shook her head.

"I happen to like your style," he said, eyeing her, his voice a low rumble. "Casual, tough. Smart and funny. Dependable. You need to laugh more, though." He disturbed the cat, setting her down before reaching over to tap between Cass's brows with a finger. "You know, erase the creases that form here sometimes."

She leaned away, rubbing the spot. She got lines there?

"You walk around frowning."

"Do not!"

"You carry a mirror?"

"No," she admitted softly, embarrassed that her fretting and freaking out was obvious to others. But honestly, if she wasn't worrying about Dusty and what was up with his heart, she was worrying about how to get the lodge up and running as soon as possible.

"And these..." He brushed the wisps of hair

trailing out of her braid, causing her to shiver. "Don't these tickle you?"

She caught her breath, struggling to focus.

"So is that a no? Not interested?" She adjusted her sweater where it was twisting around her middle, trying to get comfortable in her chair.

"I'm interested." He sat back, suddenly all business. "Would it be hard on the kids? Us staying here like a family? And then moving out again when we find a place?"

"They know we're not involved romantically," she blurted, her heart galloping.

"But when I need a date for some event, you'll be my plus one, right?" He was doing that flirtatious thing again—slow, mischievous smile, face tipped down ever so slightly.

He was pushing the envelope, trying to lighten her up, convince her to let go.

If he knew how close she was to saying yes, to leaping into his lap and kissing him, he'd surely back off. Because that was not what he wanted.

Cass paused, carefully considering her response.

Plus one. NHL star on her arm?

Yes.

But she was his nanny, so that meant she really needed to say no....

* * *

Cass was frowning at him again. She had that furious brow thing going on, which meant he'd pushed it with her. But he had to. She was so used to counting on nobody but herself that he felt he had to push past the envelope so he could get the basics.

Okay, asking her to be his date wasn't the basics.

Unless you were into her.

Was he?

She was beautiful. Easy to be around.

What was he thinking? He didn't have time for something like that, and that was not part of the agreement. Plus, she'd asked him if he wanted to stay here only for a bit and suddenly he was angling for a date instead of saying *"Heck yes! Save us from some of the commuting, woman."*

"What's that look about?" he teased. "I'll do the same for you."

"When would I ever need a date?" Cass folded her arms across her chest, the thick sleeves of her sweater bunching up. "I'm not like you. I don't have fancy events to go to."

"So I'll take that as a yes to you being my plus

one for the Christmas gala in December. Thank you."

"Landon, we're not *dating*."

"I know. I don't go for adorable, strong, fabulous women."

She rolled her eyes like he was making a dig.

"Seriously, Cass. Chill. I don't have time to be a proper, doting boyfriend. I've got to focus on my job and Rylnn. And you have—"

"This place and Dusty."

"Right."

And that giant wall around her that seemed to say *Stay Out*.

"Anyway, relationships are just so..." She sighed as though exhausted.

"Much work." He got it. "We're both busy."

Cass smiled, her shoulders dropping. "*So* much work."

"And effort. Trying to keep up with what the other person wants and needs."

"It feels like your focus is always split."

"Right?"

"And when you really need that other person," she said animatedly, "they're off doing their own thing."

"Relationships suck."

"So much." She was grinning at him, and it

was intoxicating. Was it the smile, the warmth in her eyes, or that they were connecting like this? It had been awhile since he'd felt this way.

"So? Would you be my plus one so I don't have to deal with the grind of trying to find a woman who doesn't just want to hang with celebs, and goes home with someone else?"

"Has that happened?" Cass leaned forward, her eyes boring into him for the truth.

He toyed with his teeth, running his tongue over them.

"Has it?"

"I usually just go alone."

"That's sad."

He chuckled.

"I don't do formal stuff," she said. "So even though I wouldn't go home with someone else— unless they're really hot and ask me to be *their* nanny, of course..."

"Of course."

"...I'll have to respectfully decline."

"You can't take the cowgirl off the farm?"

"Oh, you can. She loves it." Cass twisted her lips in thought. "It's just...a dress, hair, makeup, shoes, bag...I don't have any of that. Sorry." She was gazing out to the fence post, her expression slightly wistful, dusk having settled in, obscuring the yard so objects were now merely outlines.

"Speaking of helping out, if you need me to talk to Dusty about guy stuff just let me know."

"Guy stuff?"

"I don't know. Girls?"

"He's five. He still talks to his mom."

"You don't want me influencing him with all my bad-boy charm?" Landon gave her an exaggerated debonair smile.

She laughed. "You're not all bad." Her own smile was warm, full of affection.

"Thanks. You're not all bad, either."

"True."

"No news from the doctors?" he asked, referring to Dusty's still unknown heart condition.

She shook her head, that familiar forehead furrow and frown returning.

He took a sip of his cooled tea and asked, "And when Rylnn needs woman stuff, you can be that person?"

Cass laughed again, leaning closer so she could playfully smack his arm. "I knew you were angling!"

"What? Was not!"

"Were too."

"Wasn't."

"I think it's admirable. You're always looking out for her. That's a good thing, Landon. Although I think she's quite a ways away from needing 'woman' stuff."

"Kids are maturing a lot faster these days."

"Not that fast," Cass said, still laughing.

"But you understand the need she has with pretty dresses. I don't know how to get excited about them. I tried, but I fall short. What I'm saying is that Rylnn is already leaning on you, and you can lean on me. I can be that guy like you're being that gal for us."

"Be that guy?" Her cheeks were pink, though a glint of skepticism shone in her brown eyes.

"Yeah."

"Oh." Her gaze strayed in the direction of the fence post again. "Okay. Thanks."

"So? Should I get our bags then?" He leaned forward as though ready to get up should she give the word.

Cass frowned. "What? Now? You're staying?"

Landon grinned. "Just kidding. But we'll bring them tomorrow, if that's okay."

"Of course. Bring some bedding, too. And maybe a bed..."

"Anything else?"

"Anything else you can't live without, I suppose. Having enough room isn't a problem, but almost everything else is." She smiled good-naturally while gesturing to the two-thousand-square-foot building at her back. "But you need to buy your own groceries. I can only imagine what high-end items Athena has you men eating to stay in shape." Cass eyed his biceps, his thick quads.

"Fair enough."

"And I'm not cooking. You clean your own rooms and bathrooms."

"We pitch in, got it." He almost asked if he could bring his housekeeper, but figured he'd better not push it.

"And no…" Her cheeks turned red, her words hanging in the air.

"No what?"

She shrugged, as if she expected him to read her mind. He leaned closer. "No *what*, Cass?"

"No hanky-panky."

He laughed. "Hanky-panky?"

"What? I'm setting ground rules, Landon."

"No, that's fine."

"Then why are you laughing?"

"You sound like my grandma. *Hanky-panky?*"

She gave him a dark look, picked up her cup of tea and rose to her feet. Prince Charming stood as well, his head as high as Cass's ribs. The dog gave Landon a baleful look, then followed her inside.

Landon had a feeling he was really going to enjoy living here.

CHAPTER 5

$\mathcal{A}$ white box truck beeped as it backed up to Cassandra's large front door.

"What on earth?" She set down the freshly washed putty knife she'd been using to fill cracks in the upstairs hallway walls, and stepped onto the porch.

Dusty brushed past her, beelining for the cab. "Heavy-duty! Big engine!"

"Sure is," the driver said, sliding down from the tall seat.

"I'm not expecting a delivery," Cass mumbled, as the man handed her a clipboard.

"You Cassandra McTavish?"

"Yes."

"Well, I have one for you." He rolled up the

back door of the truck with a loud, rattling thump.

Prince Charming sat beside her, quietly watching. The dog didn't seem interested in guarding her or the property, and was pretty mellow, which was good with the kids around. But she figured he could at least bark or try to sniff this stranger's pant legs to let him know he was present and possibly in charge.

"Do you want to see my dress?" Rylnn called up to the truck driver as he unfolded the hydraulic lift.

Cass skimmed the delivery slip. Bed frames. Mattresses. Bedding.

"Is this for Landon Jackson?" He was fast, she'd give him that. Less than twenty-four hours after she'd made the offer, he was literally making himself at home.

The trucker whipped around. "The goalie?"

"Uh, no, just has the same name," she lied. Was his reaction what it was like having a pro hockey player in your life? Slightly unnerving.

Cass frowned at the list, not actually seeing it. She wasn't quite ready to have her life turned upside down. Then again, was having Landon living here part-time really going to change things? Probably not.

"He's my dad!" Rylnn announced proudly, thankfully not correcting Cass.

"That's nice," the driver said absently, his interest waning as quickly as it had materialized.

So far, everyone in Sweetheart Creek had been pretty laid-back about the fact that Rylnn's father was a pro athlete. Then again, the town was more about football than hockey, despite the number of NHL players that seemed to be moving here lately. Although, possibly, they were moving out here to enjoy the relative indifference and anonymity the town provided.

The deliveryman wheeled a load of boxes into the lodge's entry. She kicked a pile of shoes and boots out the of the way and directed him across the two-story, airy sitting room with the giant stone fireplace. Several bedrooms fed off the area, and Landon and Rylnn would be staying in two of them, next to Cass and Dusty's rooms. Before long, the first one was filled with mattresses and a growing pile of cartons.

"Where do you want the fridge?" the man asked after the fifth load.

Cass put down the box she'd been about to carry inside. "Fridge?"

Sure enough, there was one more large container tucked in the shadows of the delivery truck. The driver gestured to the clipboard lying on the lift. She flipped to the second page. A fridge. And at the top of the sheet was her name, same as with the bedroom items.

What on earth was Landon doing ordering a refrigerator? What was she supposed to do with the one she had? Or did he plan to keep their groceries separate, in their own fridges?

"Can you give me a minute?" She held up a finger and, pulling out her cell phone, stepped away from the truck.

Maybe the fridge was intended for Landon's place in the city. Although, truthfully, her kitchen was once a commercial cooking area and could somewhat comfortably house a second fridge, though the idea of having two seemed a tad ludicrous.

She dialed Landon. The call went to voice mail after several rings. She checked the time, realizing he was on the ice for practice.

"Rylnn?" she called.

She heard a faint answer and headed inside, finding the girl dancing. The oversize wood-burning fireplace, large enough for a witch to heat a cauldron, had a wide, raised hearthstone Rylnn loved using as a stage.

"Do you know anything about a fridge?"

"Daddy bought it for you on his iPad last night. Freezers are for freezing, Cassie. That's what he said."

"The fridge is…for me? For here?"

Rylnn continued twirling, lost in her fictional world once again.

"Careful. If you feel dizzy, get off the stone thingy, okay?" Cass eyed the four-year-old for a moment, then, shaking her head, went back outside, muttering, "He bought me a new fridge?"

Was she supposed to keep the old one? Send it away?

Or was the fridge kind of like his bed—just something he wanted while he lived here and would take with him when he left?

The driver had the giant appliance at the edge of the truck, ready to roll onto the lift and into her house.

Cass studied the box for a moment. It was huge, and the illustration on the cardboard suggested a lot of high-end features Cass hadn't realized existed.

Was Landon trying to show that he'd be full-on domestic, and that he didn't expect her to cater to him? Or was he really bothered that her fridge had frozen his precious bin of vegetables?

Whatever the reason, it gave her an odd

feeling having him buy such large things for the house, when he'd be here only until he found a place of his own.

"So? Yay or nay?" the driver asked with a hint of impatience.

"Yay?"

He grinned. "Never turn away a fancy new appliance you didn't have to pay for, that's my motto."

"Yeah. That's a good one."

What was she going to owe Landon? Anything? Her ex-husband had kept tabs, meaning a favor was never truly a favor, a gift never really a gift, as strings were always attached whether or not she could see them.

But this was different, she reminded herself several minutes later. Landon would take these things with him when he left. Which was why her old fridge was now on the back porch and Landon's was humming quietly to itself as it brought itself down to the proper temperature. She could watch the numbers falling on the LCD screen on the door and see her own reflection on its shiny surface.

"Hey!" a woman called. "You home?" Her friend Hannah's voice was followed by the sound of scrambling paws as Prince Charming hustled out to say hi. Hannah was the owner of a golden retriever, a rescue like Prince Charming, which she'd adopted after her divorce, so when her boys were with her ex she wouldn't truly be alone. Prince Charming was quite happy to give Hannah's pant legs a thorough sniffing.

"In here! Kids are out back." Cass had put the giant fridge box on the generously sized, wraparound back porch for Dusty and Rylnn, who'd vanished into it almost immediately.

Hannah said something, and then the sound of her two sons' small feet pattering across the living room's hardwood filled the house as they raced to the side door.

"What do you have here?" Hannah asked in awe when she'd joined Cass in the kitchen. She gently stroked the shiny new appliance, then opened the French doors. "Did you win the football team's 50/50 draw last week? I heard it was big."

"It's Landon's."

"He's bringing his fridge with him?" Hannah's eyes danced with amused disbelief.

"Apparently."

"Wow. Totally different caliber of boyfriend you've got yourself."

"Not my boyfriend." She'd explained the situation by text message to Hannah last night, but her friend was determined to read more into the setup than either Cass or Landon were. "He even sent bed frames and mattresses, new bedding and bedside tables." It was incredible. All new.

"Could you imagine?" Hannah said wistfully. She'd closed the fridge doors and was staring at the LCD screen.

Cass put on a posh accent, twirling her hand through the air as she spoke. "You just go online and order whatever you think you might need, and have it arrive the next day."

Hannah poked a lever, and filtered, not-quite-chilled water streamed out. She squeaked and laughed. "Sorry!"

"The kids are going to be a nightmare with this thing," Cass said, grabbing a tea towel to mop up the spill.

"There's probably a child lock."

"Which they will defeat in about ten seconds, I'm sure."

"Probably." Hannah was still stroking the appliance, tapping buttons. "It even makes ice."

Cass finished wiping away the water, then watched as her friend, braver than she was, explored and prodded the machine.

"What's all this?" Hannah squinted at the

built-in screen. She'd found a digital menu and was tapping her way through a list of options. "Connect to Wi-Fi?" She laughed. "Oh, we've got to do that!"

"Maybe it sends spoiled produce to the moon."

"Is this thing self-cleaning? You would not imagine the amount of dog hair that ends up in my fridge. Like, how? *How?*"

Giggling, they entered Cass's Wi-Fi details, then her email address for updates.

"Do you think it sends you coupons and sale notices?" Hannah asked, scrolling through a choice of grocery stores. She selected the Sweetheart Creek one. "Guess you'll find out."

"It makes grocery lists?" Cass gasped, nudging her aside as she began poking buttons, adding things to her list. Milk, bread, cereal.

"What's pomelo?" Hannah asked, as they scrolled through a fruit and vegetable menu.

"No clue."

Hannah reached past Cass and tapped on it. "If it ever goes on sale in Sweetheart Creek, you'll now get an email." She pushed the Send Order button. "Emailing your grocery list from Mr. Fancy Fridge, Ms. McTavish."

"I feel like the kids did when Cash came over with that toy kitchen he found in the town's trash-to-treasure event." Cass pulled out her phone and checked her emails. She refreshed her in-box, waiting for her grocery list to materialize. "Did you hit Send?" She glanced at the fridge screen again.

"I think so. Maybe country internet is slow."

"Maybe."

"I've got to find me a wealthy man," Hannah said with a sigh as they leaned against the counter, admiring the fridge. "Imagine all the things we're missing out on."

Cass shook her head, figuring she'd be smart not to get used to the possible luxurious perks of having Landon Jackson living under her roof.

* * *

Landon arrived in Sweetheart Creek after practice, thankful for the light afternoon on the ice—even though he and his ankle could use a few more drills in hopes of helping the team bring home a win. However, last night he'd spent hours ordering things they'd need here at Cass's, as well as packing a few bags for himself and Rylnn, and the lack of sleep was catching up with him.

As he turned down the driveway to Cass's Peppermint Lodge, the weight of the past several weeks seemed to lift from his shoulders. No hurrying back to the city tonight. They'd stay here, Rylnn in a place that already felt strangely like home. Was it because it was becoming familiar? Was it the peaceful solitude and knowledge that there wouldn't be fans outside his door in the morning?

Either way, more rest was sure to help him perform on the ice.

Eager to see if the bedroom furniture had arrived, Landon grabbed two suitcases from the back of his SUV and hustled to the front door. He walked in, calling out a hello.

"Daddy!" Rylnn squealed, screaming straight toward him. Her joy humbled him as he dropped the bags in the nick of time to catch her as she launched herself into his arms.

"Hey, sweet pea. How was your day?" He gave her a kiss on the cheek and maneuvered her onto his shoulders, her poufy dress momentarily blinding him until she got herself situated. He wandered on into the house. "Where's Cass?"

"Kitchen. She's petting the fridge."

"It came? What about your bed? Did it arrive, too?"

"I don't know," Rylnn said, lurching forward,

her cue that it was time for him to swing her down onto her feet.

"It's a princess bed," he called after her, as she headed for a side door that led to the porch and yard.

She stopped, eyes huge. "Where is it?"

"Ask Cass."

"I know!" Rylnn zipped across the large room, disappearing into one of the bedrooms Cass had pointed out to him last night.

As his daughter vanished, Cass appeared in the doorway that led to the kitchen. She was wiping her hands on a tea towel and smiling. He liked that. Smiles were a good look on her.

"Hey, I hope the delivery wasn't too much of a bother." He picked up his bags and brought them to the bedroom doorway. So many boxes. He had his work cut out for him tonight.

"It's fine, but I had the fridge sent back. I figured it was probably for your condo."

"Too late." He shot her a grin. "Rylnn already told me you love it."

"I think you're going to miss your frozen vegetables while you're staying here. But the old fridge is still on the back porch in case you're feeling sentimental."

"You didn't have it hauled away?" He was pretty sure he'd paid for that service.

She chuckled as if he was dense. "I'm going to need a fridge when you leave, you know."

"The new fridge is for you!"

"That's ridiculous."

"I'm not paying rent, unless that's a surprise you've yet to spring on me. So think of the fridge as rent."

"Then *you're* ridiculous. It's too much."

Pink cheeks. Battling a joyful smile… "But you love it, don't you?"

"Why didn't you just buy something used from in town? Why go so fancy?"

"Reduce the friction. Make it easy."

"What?"

"This is my home life. This is my foundation. I need good food, so I got a good fridge."

"Yeah, but…" She gestured back toward the kitchen.

"This is all an investment in my career, Cass. Friction adds up and slows us all down. I'm reducing friction."

Shaking her head, she followed him into the spare room where the boxes and mattresses were stacked. Landon surveyed the mound.

"There's no princess bed," Rylnn said dramatically.

Landon toed a long box. "I think this one's your frame."

"That's not a bed!"

"We have to put it together, Ry."

"Oh." She left the room, her interest dissolving.

"Is instant gratification normal at that age?" he asked Cass.

"Totally." She turned to him, hands on her hips. "Landon, that fridge is nicer than my truck."

He frowned. "Yeah, not a fair comparison."

She started sorting boxes for him, pulling out the ones that were lighter, filled with bedding.

"I had a nice truck, but a large buck that didn't understand interstate rights-of-way ended its time here on earth."

"I'm guessing the deer didn't fare much better than the vehicle?"

She winced and shook her head. "Alexa's lent me hers until I find something I like."

"And do you have to give it CPR every time you want to go somewhere?" Based on the shape of the hood, he'd guess the old Ford was from the seventies. Basically, an antique.

"Pretty much," she said casually, unbothered by the age of her ride.

She was a breath of fresh air compared to most of the people he met within his NHL circle. Although even if Cass wasn't one to take tips from someone like Cruella, the team's publicist who was all about image, she could at least maybe get a car with a safety rating from this millennium.

Someone knocked on the front door, and Cass left the room to go answer it. Landon opened the box for Rylnn's bed frame, then folded it closed again. Maybe they'd just toss the mattresses on the floor tonight.

Abandoning the task, he joined Cass at the door, where a man on the porch was holding several bags of groceries.

Prince Charming came marching in from outside, head high, one of Cass's abandoned brassieres in his mouth. Cass, turning red, tried to snatch it from him. The Great Dane latched on in surprise before reluctantly relinquishing the lingerie on command, which she then whipped out of sight.

Landon still hadn't quite figured out why her undergarments kept ending up in the yard, but he really hoped the delivery guy hadn't noticed.

The man, straight-faced, gave a nod. "I've got your order here."

Cass stepped aside, ushering Landon to the doorway.

"What's this?" He hadn't ordered groceries, at least not yet.

"Your food," Cass said.

"I didn't order any."

"Neither did I." She smiled at the courier. "Sorry." She laughed. "I didn't even know I could order all the way out here."

"New feature," he explained. "I don't think anybody's ever used it yet."

"Huh. Well, it seems we didn't, either. Are you sure you have the right place?" She reached for the slip. "Maybe I can help you find it."

The deliveryman rattled off Cass's email address, followed by, "Milk, bread, cereal. They couldn't fill the order for pomelo..."

Cass's intake of breath was so sharp Landon flinched. "What?"

She had a hand over her mouth, stifling giggles.

"What?" he repeated.

"I think I love your fridge. I don't know what any of this costs—" she accepted the bags "—but your fridge seriously just ordered food."

The man passed her a device to pay for the order.

Shaking her head, she went to find her purse. Landon pulled his wallet from his back pocket and took care of it, adding a tip as well.

He closed the door and carried the groceries into the kitchen as Cass hustled back with her debit card.

"I paid him."

"What? Why? I—"

"Yeah, I got it."

"Oh." She stopped, as though unable to process the gesture.

He put the bags on the kitchen counter. "So what happened? Something glitched?"

"No, I don't think so. Hannah and I were playing with your new fridge—"

"*Your* fridge."

"—and I think we accidentally ordered food." She was giggling again. She moved to the shiny appliance and wrapped her arms around it as best she could, like she was trying to hug it. Smiling, she said, "This must be what it's like having a wife."

Landon chuckled at her blissful expression. "I'm glad you like it."

"I think you probably need a self-cooking oven, too. Don't you think?"

"No such thing."

"Dang. How about a chef? You should probably have one here, too. Especially with your long commute. I mean, you have one in the city, right?" She began moving groceries into the fridge.

"I don't, actually. But sometimes I order a few meals from this home-cooked takeout place. They make a great vegetarian lasagna."

Cass pulled a face that made him laugh. "It's good, I promise." He handed her the last of the food and she put it away, closed the fridge, then tenderly wiped a smudge off its surface with the sleeve of her sweatshirt.

"Well, I'll believe it when I try it."

"Are you angling for me to buy you a meal?"

"Ha! And spoil me?" She was grinning when she turned to face him.

Wisps were falling out of her braid, and without thinking, he brushed one off her cheek. She was so beautiful when she smiled. It was as though she had an inner light that shone so brightly it made her entire body glow with happiness.

"Hasn't anyone ever spoiled you?" he asked,

carefully tucking a strand of hair behind her ear. She had a small stud earring at the top that he hadn't noticed before. His gaze drifted downward, curious what other details he'd missed from always being at a slight distance.

The energy of the room seemed to still. Cass blinked once. Twice.

"Nobody's spoiled you?" he whispered.

Her eyes dropped and she stepped back, her soft voice tinged with what he thought might be anger or hurt. "I grew up on a ranch where you're working too hard to spoil anyone. Then my husband left me after a difficult pregnancy and birth because he couldn't take the—" she looked up at Landon, eyes blazing with hurt and anger "—*drama*."

She shot him a careless smirk and took her polishing cloth and attacked a spot on the counter. "So, what do you think?"

Landon watched her trying to mask her pain with her scrubbing, and all he could think was that it was high time someone spoiled her rotten.

* * *

"Dusty, where's your jacket?" He was going to be late for school if he didn't get a move on.

"I hung it up."

Cass blinked at him. Her son was sprawled on his bed, flipping through a book, his school bag abandoned on the floor.

"Are you feeling okay?"

"School's boring."

She moved closer, visually checking him over. His lips were pink, there was plenty of color in his complexion and his breathing seemed fine. Having his health status hanging in limbo was wearing on her nerves.

She picked up his bag and placed it beside him. "If you hung up your coat, how did you reach the hook?"

"Landon put up my horseshoe rack."

Cass stepped to his bedroom door and glanced across the spacious sitting area to the front entry. Sure enough, his small jacket and cowboy hat were hanging there. She crossed the wide room to check it out, lifting Dusty's white hat from its hook. The rack was crafted from bent horseshoes, and had been sitting on the floor practically since the day they'd moved in. She'd marked the spot on the wall where it would go, low enough that Dusty could reach it, and then had abandoned the project.

"Is that the right spot?" Landon asked, coming

through from the kitchen, a sweating glass of water in hand. He looked refreshed and bright-eyed from his morning jog.

"Uh, yeah. It's perfect. Thank you."

"I also tightened the screws in the screen doors while I had the screwdriver out. Some of 'em were loose."

Cass gently hung the hat up again, marveling at having two items on her to-do list miraculously crossed off. Then she jangled her truck keys, calling, "Come on, little man, you don't want to be late." He'd already missed the bus.

"Did you find your lunch?" Landon asked as Dusty trudged toward them, grimacing at the idea of school. It was going to be a long haul to graduation at this rate.

"I don't like artichokes," the boy complained.

"I remembered," Landon said with a chuckle, ruffling Dusty's curly hair as he went past, his backpack nearly as big as his torso. "I promise your lunch is free of roasted artichoke dip and will be forevermore."

Cass shot him a grateful smile. Since most days Landon packed a lunch for the rink, he'd started packing Dusty's as well.

"Why can't I go to school?" Rylnn asked, climbing off the fireplace's raised hearth, where she'd been issuing royal orders to her invisible subjects.

"Next year," Landon said. "Hey, how about you slap the shaving cream on my face for me this morning?"

Rylnn squealed happily and raced for the bathroom.

They'd been at the lodge for only a week, but were settling in like they belonged. Which was worrisome. The kids would be crushed when it was time for them to move out again.

And what was Cass going to do when her gift-bearing handyman left?

Feeling grouchy, she opened the front door and whistled for the dog. Prince Charming came bounding over, his casual lope eating up the ground between them in seconds.

"Come in here, pups," she said. The Great Dane complied and Dusty slung his arms around the animal's neck.

Prince Charming was another problem. He was just a foster pet, which meant if Brant found him a home, he'd be gone.

They were building what felt like a family in a house of cards.

"Landon?" Cass called down the hall to the bathroom. "Can you make sure Prince C doesn't get out? We're leaving."

"Okay!"

"Dusty, let's go." Her son complied, and she shut the dog in the house.

She'd learned that the Great Dane, if left in the yard, would chase her truck for miles when she went anywhere. She had to either bring him along, and have him step on Dusty whenever the big dog wanted to look out the window, or to lock him in the house.

Cass climbed into the truck and watched Dusty in the rearview mirror as he got himself settled in the backseat. He looked less pale today, giving her hope that the doctors were wrong, that his heart was fine.

Even if hers might not be.

* * *

"You probably shouldn't wear that dress until I fix the hole in the armpit," Landon told Rylnn as she came dancing past him. He leaned into the bathroom, hanging his damp towel on the rack. She'd been very enthusiastic about plastering him with shaving cream, and his eyes still stung from the bits that had accidentally missed his cheeks and chin.

Rylnn lifted her arms when he turned back to her. No holes. "Cassie fixed it for me."

"That was nice of her." He found his half-drunk coffee on the bathroom counter and went to the kitchen to pour it into an insulated cup.

"She was going to wash your jersey in with her jeans, but she was afraid she'd wreck it."

"Ah." He could hear the washing machine clanging away down the hallway, already at work. "Good call. So? What are you up to today, munchkin?"

"Cassie said she'd teach me how to ride horses over at Alexa's, but we have to work on the tree corral first."

"The what?"

"Tree corral, Daddy!"

"Is she getting horses?" There was a big barn off behind the lodge, but he'd had the impression Cass was leaning toward an event center rather than returning to ranching.

"No, silly. For the Christmas trees."

"So they don't run away?"

Rylnn giggled. "We're going to make it magical."

"Yeah? How do you do that?"

"We're going to hang pretty lights above the corral. Cass says they're for weddings, but we can use them for the trees because they're almost like Christmas lights."

"And the trees go in the corral?"

She nodded. "She let Dusty and me paint the signs."

"Wow. Sounds like you've been a good helper."

"Yup. And I have myself the cowboy's boots now."

"What? You do?"

"Jenny had pink ones. Cassie says every girl needs a pretty pair of boots."

"She did, huh?" Interesting. She didn't strike him as the kind of woman who was into pretty boots. Then again, that could be because she lived in a run-down old lodge and drove a truck that was in even worse shape. She might not be able to afford them. "Who's Jenny?"

"She has a store with lots of cowgirl's stuff." Rylnn raced off, then returned with the boots.

"Is that the clothing shop next to the diner?" Landon closed his eyes, visualizing Main Street Sweetheart Creek. Blue Tumbleweed seemed like the kind of place where you might find pink cowboy boots. "And how much do I owe Jenny for your new boots?"

"I don't know!" She shrugged her shoulders, then tugged the boots on.

"Okay, so you have pink boots."

"Only for indoors."

"Only for indoors." He thought about that. "And today you're going to ride horses? In your new boots?"

"Yes."

"Outdoors?"

"Of course, silly!"

He'd let Cass figure out the whole indoor-boots-but-outdoor-riding part of the Rylnn equation.

"That sounds fun," he admitted. It had been years since he'd been on a horse. He kind of missed it, but was glad his daughter was getting to experience it.

"Daddy?"

"Yeah?"

"Can I get cowgirl's jeans like Cassie's?"

Landon froze for a second, questioning what he'd heard. "I think that would be a smart plan for horseback riding. Do you want a cowgirl shirt, too?"

"Nope."

"You sure?" She rarely ever wore the T-shirts he bought her, but he was fairly certain they still fit.

"Jeans go under princess dresses."

"Ah, I see."

Half cowgirl, half princess. He liked the impact Cass was having on his daughter. Rylnn had always been confident, but there was something new and different about her now. There was a self-assurance borne out of experience.

He half wondered if his daughter also knew how to get Cass's truck going now, too. When he'd peeked out the window earlier to see if he could release Prince Charming, he'd found the hood up, the woman half under it, Dusty in the driver's seat. The rounded view of her blue jeans hadn't been bad, and when he'd finally headed to the door to toss her the fob for his SUV, he'd heard the beast roar to life.

Grabbing his coffee, Landon took Rylnn outside, determined that this morning would be the day she learned to ride her bike without training wheels.

But instead, Rylnn begged to show him the corral first. Seeing as he was a silent investor in Cass's business, he agreed.

Cass and the kids had been busy while he'd been at games and practice. Like Rylnn had told him, the corral had white lights strung high above, and signs had been painted boasting Christmas trees for sale.

"This is very nice."

"This sign's for the driveway, and this one's for big roads."

"Very nice."

The sound of Cass's truck returning filled the air, and they headed to the front to greet her.

"Cup of coffee?" Landon asked, hoisting his insulated cup as she slid from the truck, her cowboy boots creating small dust clouds as they landed in the dirt.

"Thanks." She reached for it and took a long swallow before he could explain that he'd been offering to get her a cup of her own.

They headed inside, Rylnn's bike forgotten. Landon was unsure what Cass had planned for the day, but he was determined to be helpful in the hour he had before he left for the city.

They entered the house through the kitchen, Landon falling behind to test his screen door repair job. Not bad. Rylnn danced through the doorway, singing one of the songs from her favorite movie. Moments later, he heard a clatter and the thud of something falling—or someone.

He jogged into the kitchen to see Cass's brown hair spread out from under her giant tan dog. She was laughing, saying, "Get off! Get off me, you big lug!"

"Hey, Prince Charming, no!" Landon understood the way the dog felt. The woman was growing on him, too. But he wasn't about to knock her down and lick her face.

At least not yet.

He hauled the Great Dane off her, but she stayed where she was even after the beast was put outside. Concerned, Landon came over to see if she was okay.

"Just savoring a feeling," she said, when he gave her a questioning look.

"Wow, you need to go out on a date if cold tile and dog kisses are something you find worth savoring."

She laughed, but still didn't move.

"What kind of feeling? Numbness? Broken bones?" He was tempted to splay out next to her, curious about whatever world she was visiting down there on the chipped brown tile.

Her chest expanded as she sat up with a sigh. Landon reached for her hand and hoisted her to her feet. In cowboy boots, she was just the right height for him. Perfect.

If he was to kiss her. Which he was not.

It was just one of those thoughts that ran through his head when he found a tall woman. That was all.

"What was the feeling?" he asked, after clearing his throat.

"Nothing."

"Tell me."

"It sounds…" Her cheeks turned red. "It would make you uncomfortable."

"Now you *have* to tell me." He leaned against the counter, focused solely on her.

"You're going to think I'm nesting and that your single status is in danger."

There was a twinkle in her eyes and he laughed, knowing that she wasn't the type to corner a guy or to read too much into a situation—even one like theirs. It was one of the reasons he'd chosen her, and why he was so comfortable here.

Her eyes got a faraway look and she shrugged. "I don't know how to explain it."

"Try."

She tipped her head, glancing at him. "You know those moments you see in movies where everything is just warm and perfect?"

"Sure." He didn't, but he figured if she kept talking, it might click.

"It felt like that."

Warm and perfect?

"Happy?" he asked.

"More than that."

"Content? Secure?"

"Even more."

"Okay."

She finished his coffee and rinsed the cup.

He was curious now. Really curious. She was putting up invisible barriers, locking away what she was feeling, afraid it was too much for him. He knew she wasn't about to profess her love or anything crazy, but still…

"You won't scare me off, Cass. It's one of the things I love about staying here with you. We click. I trust you. Same wavelength and all that. Ry and I are happy and content, too."

She shifted impatiently, as if he wasn't listening. "Better get ready to run," she murmured, keeping her back to him.

He moved to the sink, then leaned against the counter, facing her. "Already ran this morning. What is it? You want to have my babies?" He gave her a light nudge.

"Yeah, of course. Who doesn't?" Her dry tone left his ego dented. What had he expected her to say?

She half turned, one hand on the counter's edge, and waved around the kitchen with the other one. "It feels like marriage. Family. We're a family."

"Acting like one."

She added quickly, "I know. I'm not putting any of that on us and this situation. It's just…I haven't felt secure like that since I was a kid. This morning felt like…family. It was nice. That's all."

She wouldn't quite meet his eyes.

"It's okay, Cass." He gave her shoulder a light massage. "You already warned me. I expect entrapment and am prepared to evade it."

She reached out to give him a playful whack, but he caught her arm, drawing her close. For a second, he almost pulled her against him for a kiss, as if it was an old habit of theirs. Instead, he tugged her in for a hug.

"Little do you know, you're already trapped," she mumbled against his chest. "Two kids, a dog, me. All under one roof." She glanced up at him, her grin wicked. "And I've secretly told everyone in town not to rent to you, so you can never escape."

"Works for me. We like it here."

"It does work, doesn't it?" She was leaning back, no longer in his arms, brave enough to look him in the eye.

He nodded.

"I know it sounds crazy, but I always thought I'd have this feeling. You know? Just assumed this was how my marriage was going to feel. Easy."

"But it didn't?" He noticed she never spoke about Dusty's dad, not even when talking about the medical bills.

She shook her head. "No. But that's okay. I wouldn't have had this morning."

But in her marriage, surely there had been moments like this morning? Better moments. More of them before things had dissolved, right?

She smiled, and he could see it in her. Something had shifted. Him being here and doing small things around the place, Rylnn serving as her shadow—even with everything going on with Dusty—it was all good for her. Healing somehow.

This was where he was supposed to be. Him and Rylnn.

"Anyway, I was just breathing it in. I didn't mean to scare you."

"Not at all." Not in the least. Because something was shifting inside him, too. He just wasn't sure what it was yet and if there was a word for it.

CHAPTER 6

"The Christmas trees weren't supposed to arrive for at least another week," Cass muttered to herself. She stormed into the house, slamming the screen door behind her. They were jam-packed in their crates and it had taken her an hour to unpack the first crate of six sitting in her yard.

Her arms already itched from the tiny pine needle scratches that her thick flannel shirt had been unable to protect her from.

Time had gotten away from her and she had only an hour to fix the kids' costumes for trick-or-treating, as well as figure out what to feed them for supper. If it were just herself and Dusty, they'd have cereal, but being paid to care for

Rylnn kind of upped the game and removed the option of some of her less than fabulous parenting shortcuts. The ones she'd never admit to another person for fear of judgment.

Cass stopped beside the fireplace to resettle her mind and figure out how she was going to triage this evening. Too many problems, not enough solutions.

Alexa's stupid old truck had died on her between the doctor's office in San Antonio and home. It had been a rough morning even before then, with the doctor's news and the kids' meltdowns, but if she thought about any of that now she might start crying.

Solutions. She needed to focus on making sure Halloween didn't become ruined for the children.

Landon should be back from practice in time to drive them into town for trick-or-treating. The Christmas trees could wait in their travel crates until after that.

And they were having cereal for supper.

She sucked in a steadying breath, fighting the urge to check on Dusty, even though she knew he was okay. Today's appointment had not brought the good news she'd wanted, and a panicky sensation enveloped her whenever she thought about the visit. Dusty's doctor had gently suggested that the kids play outside his office while he brought in a pediatric surgeon who specialized in cardiology, so they could discuss the possibility of heart surgery.

Breathe.

They needed more tests first. More research. More consulting with other pediatric cardiologists.

Breathe.

Time to focus on the here and now. Halloween. Find the glue gun and fix Rylnn's massive cardboard crown, which they'd been working on all week. Help Dusty make new bat-throwing star things for his Batman costume.

The doctors had told her his status wasn't urgent. That he'd be fine if he didn't exert himself with a lot of running around—which he didn't seem very apt to do anyway, due to his fatigue.

She rubbed her arms again, her attention drifting to the mantel. Something was different about the lineup of family photos.

A framed picture of Dusty as a baby, lying on his stomach, smiling toothlessly.

She and Alexa as teens, laughing at the camera.

Dusty sledding in Montana, cheeks rosy from the cold.

And something new: a hand-drawn picture done in colored markers. It had been folded over the framed photo of Cass on a horse, taking a place of honor.

She lifted the drawing from the mantel, careful not to mess with how it was folded around the frame. Lots of pinks and blues and yellow, and a giant sun in the right-hand corner that was Rylnn's calling card. Four stick figures: two tall, two short. One of the tall figures was blue and had a hockey stick. The other was drawn in pink and wore a cowboy hat. Between them stood two smaller figures, one in a princess dress and one in a cowboy hat. All four were holding hands.

A family.

With shaking fingers, Cass returned the drawing to the mantel, blinking away the sudden moisture in her eyes.

What Rylnn wanted wasn't wrong. Cass wanted it, too. Someone who balanced her out, like Alexa had found in her husband. They made it look easy, and Cass knew from experience that love and marriage were anything but. At the end of the day, Alexa was never rowing that boat of hers alone because Cash was there, ready to take the oars when she needed a break.

And since Cass knew just how rare that was, she was more than happy to savor her pretend family and Landon's help—even if only for a few weeks.

* * *

Landon entered the kitchen from the side yard, finding Cass hunched over a glue gun. She looked up, delight sparking in her eyes.

"You're home?" She quickly checked the clock over the stove before she resumed her work, brow furrowing in concentration.

"I thought I'd missed trick-or-treating. Where's your truck?"

"Dead."

He stepped closer, inhaling the sweet pine smell that filled the space. "What are you up to? And why do you smell like you've been rolling around in a forest?"

When she looked up from her task again, her gaze unfocused, he realized she was frazzled.

"What?" she asked.

He pulled a pine needle from her braid. Her

Christmas trees must be in the crates lined up by the corral. "Can I help with anything?"

"No, I've got it."

"Have the kids eaten?"

"No, I'm sorry." She waved toward the cupboard. "There's cereal."

He watched her out of the corner of his eye as he ignored the breakfast cupboard and checked the fridge's contents, then began prepping grilled cheese sandwiches.

"So your truck's dead?"

"Cash and Nick are looking it over."

Nick was Alexa and Cash's ranch hand, if he recalled correctly. His girlfriend, Polly, ran the rescue horse portion of the ranch or something like that. She was from Canada, too—the one time he'd met her they'd mostly cracked jokes about the Great White North, but he hadn't really had the chance to find out more about her or what she did over at Blueberry Creek Ranch.

"What are you driving in the meantime?" Landon asked Cass.

She'd been taking Rylnn to story hour at the library, drop-in dance lessons and even a few play dates, but all that would stop if she had no wheels.

She shrugged, the muscles in her shoulders

tightening. "I'll figure something out." She held up the crown she and Rylnn had been working on for days. "What do you think? Can you tell it got smashed in an elevator today?"

An elevator? "Oh, yeah! Hey, how was Dusty's appointment? I meant to ask first thing." How had it slipped his mind? He'd been thinking about the boy all day, knowing that this appointment would determine whether Dusty needed surgery.

Cass shook her head, dropping her eyes as she swept glitter from the counter into her cupped hand. "Rylnn! Crown's done!"

"It's done?" Rylnn asked, hopping into the room.

"Check it out." Cass passed her the fixed costume piece.

Rylnn placed it on her head. "It's beautiful." She spun, then stopped in the kitchen doorway, hollering so loud she bent over, "Dusty! It's your turn!"

"His turn for what?" Landon asked, tossing buttered bread into the hot pan, then layering on sliced cheese.

"Fixing his costume."

"What's wrong with it?" When Landon had left that morning, both kids had been decked out, beaming and proud of their costumes, ready for their trip to the city. It sounded like it had been a rough day all around.

"He threw his Batman's stars out the window," Rylnn answered. "Auntie Lexa wouldn't turn back for them."

"She didn't hear him," Cass said, the frazzled fatigue Landon had noted earlier returning.

"You were with Alexa?" Landon asked.

"She rescued us."

"From the side of the road?"

"It was so *boring*." Rylnn sighed.

"Dusty! Come in here if you want to make new stars." Cass turned to Landon. "How long until sandwiches?"

"Five minutes," he said, checking the bread's white underside. "When does trick-or-treating start?"

"We're meeting at Hannah's at a quarter after six so I can borrow a dress. Do you have a costume?"

He glanced at the clock. They were going to have to inhale supper to make it to town on time.

"I'll wear a jersey and drive us in. Tomorrow, I'll catch a ride with Maverick so you can use the SUV."

"No, no. I'll borrow something of Alexa's if we need to go somewhere."

"It's not a problem for me to carpool until you find a replacement."

"I'm not buying a new truck right now." The stress lines around Cass's mouth returned.

"I'm hungry," Dusty said, entering the kitchen, his black Batman cape—made from one of Landon's old T-shirts—swirling behind him.

"Landon's making sandwiches."

Dusty, grinning at him, grabbed something from his costume's utility belt and whipped it forward. It fluttered through the air, landing at Landon's feet.

"Where's the cardboard?" Cass asked. "We'll make you new batarangs."

"Ow!" Landon hopped as if Dusty's weapon had hit him. "Holy cow, Batman! What was that? I told you I'm not The Joker! I'm innocent. I'm just a goalie. A hockey player! I'm a friend of Gotham City!" He pretended to be scared, throwing himself behind Cass, grabbing her shoulders and swinging her like a shield between himself and Dusty.

The little boy giggled, trying to get to him with a piece of painted cardboard the size of his palm.

"What is that?" Landon clung to Cass. "Save me, Catgirl."

Cass giggled. "I'm not Catgirl."

"She's *Cowgirl!*" Rylnn announced, running back into the room, her flowing pink dress glimmering under the kitchen lights. "And I'm the Boss Princess!" She twirled what looked like an invisible lasso at Cass, who pretended to snatch it from the air.

Cass twisted out of Landon's grip like someone well-versed in self-defense. After throwing Rylnn's "lasso" at Batman, she leaped across the room, grabbed her son and locked him in her arms.

Landon, laughing, lifted Boss Princess in the air. "We saved the day!"

"I'm a good guy!" Dusty yelled. He slipped from his mom's grip, then turned to point at her.

"No running, Dusty!" Cass warned.

"*She's* the bad guy!" he said, halting in his tracks. "Get her, Blockade!"

"I'm on it!" Landon set Rylnn down and dropped into a ready stance, arms out, as Cass squealed and mimicked his posture. "Nobody gets past me. I'm The Blockade."

Her eyes widened dramatically in false alarm.

"What's our plan, Boss Princess?" he said to Rylnn, not taking his attention from Cass.

"Get her!" Rylnn lifted her arm as if shooting a starting pistol.

Landon lunged at Cass who, laughing, dodged him, pushing open the screen door and running out onto the porch. Prince Charming, who'd heard the commotion, barked at Landon when he came out after her.

"It's okay, PC!" He dashed past the dog, Rylnn hot on his heels.

"Careful!" Cass called.

The whole yard smelled like evergreens and Landon inhaled, brought back to days on his grandma's ranch when Chinooks would come down the mountains. The warm air, a thousand miles from the coast, would eat up the snow, changing the temperature from frigid to balmy within a few hours.

Home.

He caught up with Cass at the corral. She'd unpacked a few Christmas trees earlier, and had leaned them against the wide wooden fence. She darted behind the rails at the opening, her back to a seven-foot pine, its branches bound up with twine.

"I have you now!" he sang.

Landon lunged at her and several kittens went scurrying out from under the trees. Just as his fingers touched her, his feet went out from under him and he fell forward. Cass gasped, the dog barked and the tree slipped from its vertical position, taking them with it, softening their fall with a loud crack of branches as they landed on top of it.

Cass's eyes and mouth went wide in surprise. The Great Dane reached past Landon with his giant head, slurping his tongue up the side of Cass's cheek. She started giggling, her beautiful face bright with joy.

Landon's body was pressed to hers, her hands against his chest. He lifted his torso, relieving her of some of his weight. "Are you okay?" he asked, unable to move as both kids piled on top of them, and for the simple fact that he really didn't want to.

* * *

As Landon carefully shifted his body off of her, Cass felt the absence of his weight securely pinning her in place. He had been warm, comfortable and solid. For a moment she'd been in a safe cocoon, his heart beating against her chest, their breathing in sync.

The Christmas tree beneath her cracked in

protest again as Landon pulled her to her feet. She dusted herself off, and when Prince Charming nudged her with his nose she bent and wrapped her arms around his neck, ruffling his short fur to soothe him. The chase across the yard and subsequent tumble had him all stirred up.

"Uh-oh." Landon was grimacing, his eyes on the ground.

Cass looked at the tree that had cushioned their fall. Despite it being protectively bound in twine, the surrounding area was littered with needles, and broken branches protruded from the bundle like compound fractures.

"Oh dear!" She matched Landon's grimace, then laughed. "Well, I'd planned to keep a tree for us. I guess this is the one."

She giggled again, and Landon chuckled beside her, draping his arm around her as they started back to the house, the kids already well ahead of them.

"You okay?" he asked.

"I am, thanks."

"I think PC is protective of you, after all."

Cass smiled up at Landon, enjoying the comfort of having his big arm flung over her shoulders.

"The sandwiches are burning!" Dusty hollered from the kitchen door. The dog barked and tore into the house.

"Get firefighters!" Rylnn screamed.

After a quick, shared look of alarm with Cass, Landon ran to the door, his right ankle stiff and causing him to hobble momentarily. He was in the kitchen before she even reached the porch, his training on the ice making him a fast sprinter. When she entered the kitchen, he was waving smoke away from the pan, the smoke detector blaring. The dog spun and raced back out through the screen door, sending it banging against the porch wall.

Landon tipped the pan, sliding the sandwiches onto a plate. Two went skittering off into the air and onto the floor.

Cass pinched them between her fingers, then tossed them onto the counter with a grimace. The sandwiches were white on one side, black on the other. Carefully, she pulled back the burned bread to see what could be salvaged.

"Think the Longhorn has anything Athena-approved on the menu?" Landon mused.

"I'm sure we can scrounge up something here," Cass said, tossing the sandwiches into the dog's food dish.

"Nope. I give up," Landon declared, dusting his hands together.

"We're adults. We're not allowed to give up," she stated.

"We can."

"Landon…"

"Too much friction. It's a sign to take the easy route and enjoy our night."

Cass blinked. "The easy route?"

When was there ever an easy route?

He directed her to the front door, hands on her shoulders. She relaxed, letting him push her along. It felt nice to have someone else making decisions, solving problems. It didn't hurt that his thumbs were circling absently around the tight muscles of her shoulder blades.

She could get used to this. Really, really used to this.

CHAPTER 7

*L*andon and Cass trailed after the kids on the busy sidewalks of Sweetheart Creek as night folded in around them. Cass had donned a gown that was sorely out of fashion, as well as one of Rylnn's toy tiaras. Not having any high heels, she wore her best boots, which, much to Landon's surprise, had passed his daughter's stringent princess-costume checklist.

But even more surprising was the way Cass carried herself. He'd believed, at first, that she was dressing up just to make Rylnn happy. But seeing how she stood tall in her fancy outfit, Landon believed Cass might have a bit of an inner princess.

Personally, he wasn't dressed much differently

from when he was on the ice, save for a few absent bits of gear. Rylnn had commanded him to wear a jersey, gloves, helmet, and carry a hockey stick. He didn't mind, really. He loved the kids' excitement as they tore from door to door, their treat bags growing plumper as the night wore on. And the folks of Sweetheart Creek didn't hound him, just the odd person or kid asking for a selfie or autograph. Not bad at all.

"You need less friction in your life," Landon said to Cass during a moment alone with her. He'd noticed that the tension she'd been carrying in her muscles had lifted as soon as he'd started making the sandwiches, and then again after he'd taken them all to the diner, asking Mrs. Fisher to put a rush on their order.

The whole nanny-and-living-with-each-other thing was going well, but they had no timeline for their agreement. He wanted permission to step up and step in more like he had tonight. He wanted to know where his place was, and what he could do within their makeshift family unit without overstepping. He wanted to know his boundaries so he didn't accidentally blow it for the four of them.

"We need to create less friction for you."

"Yeah," Cass muttered, her eyes not moving

from Dusty, who was falling behind with each block, unable to keep up with Rylnn, who was spinning like an out-of-control top.

Cass's friend Hannah was doing a valiant job of keeping the kids together, her own sons, Wade and Thomas, waiting for Dusty and roping in Rylnn as needed.

"Dusty, you need a piggyback ride?" Landon asked when they caught up with him.

"I'm okay."

Cass cupped his chin, her own expression serious. "Take it easy, okay?"

Dusty nodded and headed up the next driveway, while Landon and Cass hung back. "He all right?" Landon asked, tipping his head in Dusty's direction.

She nodded tightly and adjusted the skirt of her dress. When the two women had stepped out of Hannah's house, dressed for trick-or-treating, Landon hadn't known whether to laugh or gawk. The laughter would be for Hannah's costume—brown leggings, shirt and hat all covered with inflated purple balloons to make her look like a bunch of grapes. Her eldest son, Wade, had her red-faced, sneaking in to pop her balloons while she darted away.

Cass, however, had looked gorgeous despite

the ridiculously dated blue dress with puffy sleeves, tight waist and big skirt that fell about a foot too short. Her hair was up, smoothed and covered in glitter, and subtle makeup brought out the shape of her eyes. She'd left him speechless. Apparently he had a thing for eighties' princesses. Who knew?

"What can I do to help out more?" he asked, snapping back to the present as they walked through the town, following their trick-or-treaters.

"Nothing." She lifted her shawl higher on her shoulders. "You've done plenty."

"The fridge is just a tool—something to keep my precious, prescribed meals from freezing before I can eat them."

She smiled. "You know you're taking the fridge with you, so it doesn't count. I meant stuff like covering Dusty's hospital bill."

"Also doesn't count. All part of the deal." The medical bill, after Cass's insurance was done with it, hadn't been that much more than the fridge.

"To me it counts."

"Then you're welcome."

She turned to him, her eyes serious under the streetlights. "Thank you. Did I not say that already?" She gripped his arm. "I'm sorry. I really appreciate it, Landon." Her hand was warm through his jersey, despite the chill in the late October air. It felt nice. Connected.

She released him, and he immediately missed her physical touch.

"There are more bills coming?" He watched her as they walked, knowing that today hadn't gone well. They might not have known each other for a long time, but he was learning to read her as if they'd been friends forever.

"There are more bills coming," she echoed, her steps slowing. "The doctors say surgery."

"Heart surgery?" Landon's gaze shot to Dusty in his Batman costume. So small, so vulnerable. It was unthinkable, the idea of such an intrusive, serious operation on such a fun-loving child.

Cass nodded bleakly.

Landon rested a hand on top of his helmet, trying to contain his thoughts. "When? How much does your insurance cover?"

"I don't know yet."

"This really sucks."

"I know."

"And you need a new truck."

Cass's strides grew longer, her pace increasing.

Landon caught up to her and grasped her

hand. He gave it a squeeze, then tried to pull his hand back in case people took it to mean something, but she held on tight. He gave another squeeze, wishing she'd let him do more for her and her son.

They stopped at a driveway, waiting while the kids went up to the next door. Small bodies brushed past them like they were a solitary island, joyous calls of "trick-or-treat!" filling the night air.

"We should form a family unit," he whispered to Cass. A solid team, taking on the world together. Raising their kids, pooling their skills and resources.

Hannah turned to say something about how cute the kids were, and Cass whipped her hand out of Landon's. Her friend's eyes grew round before she turned away again.

"Landon, I'm not… We're not—this isn't…"

"No, I know," he said quickly, embarrassed at how flustered and upset she was.

"Something like that could complicate things. In a big, bad way."

"That's not what I meant. Neither of us is interested in something romantic," he said with false calmness. "I meant like a team. Look at us tonight. We tag-teamed the problems."

"Because you threw money at them."

"Just supper."

"I can't throw money at our problems."

"I'm not asking you to. Tonight you used a glue gun, humor, love and patience. You have a steady parenting vibe. Rylnn is thriving. Money didn't help that brewing parenting issue. *You* solved it—are solving it—just by being you. Your resources are different than mine, and I'm suggesting we lean into what we can each contribute."

Cass was frowning under the streetlight, her freckles disappearing in the folded scrunches of her nose. It was adorable.

He winced, realizing that he was basically proposing something traditional. Man goes out into the world and gets the bacon. Woman stays home with offspring.

"Actually, maybe it's a stupid idea. Just forget it. We can keep it a professional relationship, with no blurred edges just because we're raising kids under the same roof."

She was shaking her head, brow furrowed in thought. "No, I think I see what you're getting at." Landon breathed in relief at her warm, slow smile. "You're going to be my sugar daddy."

They both burst out laughing.

He poked her side, sending her into giggles. "You know that's not what I'm proposing."

"I know," she said, recovering. "We'd each bring what we have to the table to raise our little hooligans. Like we already are, only with fewer professional boundaries, and more chipping in whenever we see a need. Like friends. Roommates. Is that what you mean?" She turned to him, her eyes dark and serious.

He nodded.

"But this could end up lasting for years?"

He shrugged and nodded.

They paused as the kids cut across their path, Wade and Thomas trying to convince Dusty to give them the candy he didn't like.

Up ahead Hannah had stopped to chat with the woman from the shelter who dropped off dog food for PC—April Wylder.

Cass turned her face away from her gossiping friends. She was pretty with her hair done up in the princess do, tendrils dancing over her exposed collarbone. He took in her expression, realizing she was frowning again.

"What?"

She stepped closer, saying quietly, "Rylnn drew a picture of the four of us holding hands. She put it on the mantel with my family photos.

Are we going to mess up the kids if we start acting like we're a…family?"

"Family are the people you choose, Cass."

His attention strayed to Cass's glittery pink tiara. Princess Cowgirl. The woman he hoped his daughter became. Independent, but also unafraid to step into her beauty. Own it. All of it. Everything from her smarts to her looks.

"If we don't do this right," Cass warned, "when you leave, it might end up feeling like a divorce."

"That won't happen," he said. "Because it's just business. Both you and I know that."

And yet the niggling feeling that he was lying refused to be tamped down.

* * *

Cass zipped into Hannah's to return the borrowed dress. She ducked into the bathroom there, then opened the door again and stuck her head out. "Hannah? Can you unzip me?"

She heard the loud popping of balloons and saw Hannah's dog, Obi, go flying past in a panic. Her friend was giggling, and obviously busy with her own costume now that her boys were off with their dad, to drop by the in-laws for more Halloween treats.

Sighing, Cass padded across the wood floors of Hannah's old cabin to the front door to find Landon.

Trick-or-treaters waylaid her, and she deposited candy in their bags before waving to Landon, who was in his SUV, parked in the short driveway. She beckoned to him.

He opened the door and called, "What?"

"Come here!"

"Why?"

"Just come!" Cass called back.

He climbed out and jogged up the steps, agility personified. She could still feel his athletic body flattening hers with its comforting, secure weight only a few hours ago. The intimacy of a few stolen seconds where she could pretend they were in love. That everything was real, and not just two struggling parents clinging to each other like life rafts.

She turned, saying over her shoulder, "Can you unzip me?"

"Seriously, Cass?"

"What? I'm stuck!"

"Mere minutes after agreeing to blur the boundaries of our deal you've got me undressing you?"

She laughed at his teasing, still elated at how

easy things were between them, at how they were supporting each other so they could be better parents.

Where had he been all her life?

His hands were warm on her neck while he fiddled with the small latch, then the zipper. She shivered at the contact, then inhaled sharply as cold air rushed against her bare back.

"How far down?" he asked.

"That's good." She reached around for the zipper tab, realizing he was likely getting a nice view of the top band of her undies.

Before she stepped away, he lightly traced a finger up her spine, sending chills through her body. She spun around, holding the dress tight to her torso. "Landon!"

His grin was wide, his eyes bright with mischief. He gave an innocent shrug and hopped down the steps. She shook her head, watching him go, unable to remain upset. She knew he meant nothing by it, but it sent her into a tizzy, thinking things she really shouldn't.

Back in the bathroom, she shucked off the dress and exchanged it for her jeans and an orange sweater.

"Hannah?" she called, shaking out the gown. "I'm leaving. Thanks for loaning me the costume."

"At least it still fits someone," her friend answered, coming out of her bedroom. "I can't believe your waist is still that small after having a baby. Mine tripled in size, I swear." Her voice dropped an octave. "Hey, things were looking...*interesting*...with you and Landon tonight."

Cass gave her a serious frown, hoping to distract her from noticing her burning cheeks. "I'm his daughter's *nanny*."

"Right," she replied in a skeptical tone.

"Seriously, Hannah. How stereotypical and sad would it be if we started doing something *interesting* together?"

"You're too old for that nanny-rich-man story." Hannah paused to think. "Maybe you're just two single parents looking for a good time?" She lifted her brows, waiting for confirmation.

Cass snorted. "It's not like that."

"Sure, sure."

Cass tried to find the words to explain that they were just two single parents leaning on each other. But why would a man like Landon, with money and fame, come all the way out into the country to live in a tired old lodge just so she could be Rylnn's nanny? People would never believe it.

She barely did.

What if they believed he was using her situation to his advantage? That Cass was providing *favors* in exchange for financial help?

Even though her friend was also a single mom, Cass wasn't sure if she'd see the mutuality of the agreement she and Landon had. Hannah was still really close with her ex, Calvin, and they were co-parenting like a dream. Whereas Cass hadn't seen her ex in years.

The last thing she wanted was the townsfolk twisting things around and bringing either of them—or the kids—shame. Dusty had to grow up here. He didn't need people speculating that his mom was working as a kept woman in order to provide for him.

"I saw you two holding hands."

Cass bit down on her smile. His reaching out for her had felt nice. The way he recognized her had felt right. Like a shelter appearing in a thunderstorm, shielding her.

"Speaking of Landon, I'd better run."

"We're going to talk about this!" Hannah called after her.

With a bounce in her step, Cass jogged out to the SUV and popped into the passenger seat.

"Everybody ready?" Landon asked, glancing over his shoulder at their kids.

"Ready!" Cass called, putting on her seat belt.

"Ready!" chimed Dusty and Rylnn from the backseat.

Landon put the car in reverse and placed his hand on the passenger seat headrest, watching Cass while he waited for a family to clear the sidewalk so he could back out.

"What?" She felt a self-conscious warmth spread across her face, as if he could read her mind. Because maybe they should let the town think they were in a relationship. It was easier than trying to explain that they weren't.

"Need help with those trees once we get home?" he asked.

"You must be tired. Didn't you say Louis was going to bag skate you all today because of the team's losing streak?"

Landon grinned. "He did. But as goalie, it's never as bad, since he needs someone in net for some of his bag-skating drills."

He was still looking at her, his expression warm, welcoming, friendly.

"What?" She smoothed her hair, forgetting Hannah had done it up for her with a million pins, a gallon of hair-spray and a fistful of glitter.

"Never seen a woman in makeup before?" She batted her lashes and swiveled a shoulder, enjoying the opportunity to flirt, to feel like she was worthy of a second glance.

"Yes, but not on you," he whispered, backing up the vehicle with care. "You look nice."

The way the words slipped from his lips like a confession she wasn't supposed to hear made her want to buy out the cosmetics aisle at the Sweetheart Creek drugstore.

Maybe she could ask Daisy-Mae Ray, the town's former beauty queen, to give her a crash course in how to be gorgeous.

What was she thinking?

This was dangerous.

Flirting? Fishing for compliments? Trying to find out whether Landon found her attractive?

She was going to sink this cohabitation, co-parenting thing before the ship even left the harbor.

Landon was a nice guy. A nice guy with needs that she could fulfill—as a *nanny*. She had to lock down her libido, or her ever-suffering self-esteem and its need for affirmation, or whatever it was that kept rearing up right now. They were a family unit.

Family.

And not in the traditional romantic sense.

Because that, she knew, involved love. And love was not in the cards.

* * *

After the kids had settled enough that Landon could read them their bedtime story, he tucked them in, then wandered through the large house, wondering where Cass had disappeared to.

And not because unzipping her dress, exposing her bare back inch by inch, had affected him earlier and he longed to be around her, like a moth drawn to a porch light.

Well, maybe it was partly because of that, but also because of habit. He couldn't hear her talking on the phone any longer, her earlier call to her ex-husband having been unexpectedly abrupt and terse. He continued to look for her, thinking she might want to sit by the fire and have a cup of peppermint tea, as it was too dark to work on her trees. Their practice of sitting on the porch each evening had moved inside due to the late autumn chill, but he found it just as relaxing as being outdoors.

Although tonight his attention might continually drift to wondering whether she had other outfits she needed help getting out of, and what it might take to find her stuck in another one—and in need of his assistance to remove it.

Cass had several projects on the go, and when Landon didn't find her in the kitchen or scraping wallpaper in the powder room, he headed upstairs to see if she was fixing wall cracks in the loft area.

She was determined to get the wedding center up and running without taking on debt, which meant a lot of sweat equity. She was equally determined to pay every medical bill, which meant, with the blurring of their agreement's lines, he was going to have to get creative in the ways he helped her out.

On a whim, when he didn't find her in the loft, he checked the already-stripped old smoking room overlooking the yard's small pond and wooded area beyond.

He wanted to talk to her about Dusty's upcoming surgery, and how the boy had gone down for the night much easier than Rylnn, despite being hopped up on sugar. He'd crashed during the first page of the story, and Landon had carried him to his room.

Still looking for Cass, Landon headed downstairs to find Prince Charming at the back door, ears perked. Landon pushed aside a gingham curtain and peered out the half window. Cass was out there, working on her trees in the dark.

Quickly changing into jeans and a flannel jacket, Landon joined her outside the corral, where she was trying to pry the side off of a huge, loosely made wooden crate. Through the slats he could see her Christmas trees, packed tightly, each coiled in twine.

He paused, watching her. The peaceful feeling that had enveloped her earlier was gone. She was cursing under her breath as she wielded the crowbar, muttering awful things that would have made the guys on the hockey bench blush.

Well, not quite. They had quite the mouths when given the opportunity to express themselves—and they'd had plenty to express this season thanks to their crappy, record-breaking losing streak.

A nail shrieked in protest as Cass reefed on the crowbar. He moved up beside her, the scent of her laundry soap mingling with the pine. He gently took the tool from her, and she let out a shaky breath.

"I've got this," he said. "Why don't you put the trees where you want them as I free them?"

She didn't step away, and he could see her

fighting the urge to take out her frustrations on the crate.

"Go," he said.

"Stupid nails."

"You're used to the world bending to your will, aren't you?" he teased.

"Yes! And that crate is impossible! I'm going to go borrow a chainsaw from Cash."

"Just hang on a sec, okay?" Landon pried a board off, then another, opening enough of the crate for her to free the trees.

"Stupid sexual dimorphism. I could use more testosterone."

"Ew. Please no. You're perfect the way you are."

"Incapable! Weak! You made that look easy!" Grumbling, she started moving trees, giving each one a shake as if it was out of line for not breaking free on its own.

Wise enough to give her time and space, Landon began working on the rest of the crates. The yard light cast a glow, the darkness of the night fully surrounding them like they were performing on a stage, everything else hidden in shadows. When he'd opened several more he peered into the corral, checking her progress. The trees she'd leaned against the rails blocked most of the light from the yard, casting long, impenetrable shadows. In the faint light he couldn't make out her organizational system, and the strings of lights that crisscrossed above weren't plugged in to help illuminate the area.

Landon walked the perimeter of the corral, looking for a switch or outlet. No extension cord, and he wasn't sure where Cass kept them, or if she had one long enough to reach from the house. Not wanting to add another problem to her pile, he headed for the house, grabbed his keys and soon had the SUV positioned so the headlights shone into the corral, chasing away the shadows.

Wordlessly, he brought two trees to the entrance for Cass to put away.

She sniffed as he drew near, her work glove dashing across her face. It wasn't until she sniffed again that he realized she was fighting tears.

"Cass?"

She gave a shake of her head.

"Come here." He pulled her against him and pressed her head to his shoulder, stroking her hair. In the glow from his headlights the glitter from her fancy princess up-do sparkled and fell, like fairy dust being sprinkled around them. After a long moment he leaned back and peered down at her damp face. "What is it?" he asked.

The tears streamed faster. She gave a strangled hiccup.

"Cass, you can tell me."

She shook her head, unable to speak, her hands fisting his jacket. He tucked her against him again trying to anchor her.

"It's nothing," she finally mumbled through her sniffles.

"I have the feeling it's everything, isn't it?"

She shoved against his chest, but not hard enough to push him away, while looking up at him with such a forlorn expression he wondered how anyone could ever say no to her.

"Why are you so nice to me?"

"Who *isn't* being nice to you? Your ex-husband?" Landon demanded, a sudden urge to protect her overcoming him. He'd learned some good fighting moves on the ice. He was fit. Fast. He could take the man. "Where does he live?"

She laughed at his expression, the mirthful sound short and choked, then sniffed again, shaking her hands to knock off her work gloves so she could wipe her wet face.

Her gloves had left dirt streaks earlier, and her pretty makeup was a mess. Landon peeled off his own gloves, then took the hem of his shirt, lifting it high while carefully cradling her head with his free hand. He gently dabbed at her tears, then, using the wet fabric, swept away the blur of mascara under her lashes and the dirt smudges on her cheeks. Unable to help himself, he traced along the edge of her lower lip, tidying her now-faded lipstick. She had beautiful full lips, and a soft smile that always felt generous, but often vanished too quickly.

"It's going to stain your shirt," she said, her eyes welling again.

"Is that really what you're worrying about?" he asked, giving her a half smile. When she smiled back, hers wobbly and weak. "Dusty?"

Her eyes filled with tears. Cass bit her bottom lip and nodded.

"You know you can lean on me," he said, making sure she met his gaze, saw the sincerity of his words.

"Why *are* you so nice?"

"You prefer to hang out with jerks?" he countered.

"I seem to attract them."

"Hey!" he protested, trying to lighten the mood. "I'm right here, Cass."

She blinked slowly. "That's not what's going on here."

"Right." No attraction. Casual family-unit agreement.

He was surprised by the stab of disappointment that had landed in his solar plexus. It was like a hard hit with the end of a hockey stick when he'd been looking the other way.

She straightened her shoulders. "It's a platonic relationship."

Relationship? Why was it like someone turned a light on behind a door he'd firmly, stubbornly been ignoring? And now streaks of light beckoned to him from underneath the closed portal like a promise, even though it had a giant Do Not Enter sign on it.

"Landon?"

She was waiting for him to confirm her words.

"Yeah, I *know*, Cass."

CHAPTER 8

"What is this?" Cass asked, holding on to the screen door like it was an anchor into reality. A reality where, if she didn't fully step outside, the shiny new truck in the driveway would make sense.

Landon tossed her a fob.

Cass stepped onto the porch to catch the piece of fresh black plastic. A beautiful green truck. New. Four-door. Not a scratch or a smudge on it.

Her brain was screaming *No*.

"Landon?" Her tone held a warning that would probably send shivers up the spines of every man within a five-mile radius.

"Go on, check it out."

"Landon." Things had been going good—no,

amazing—with them sharing duties around the house and with the kids. Tag-teaming like they'd been born to co-parent.

So what was he doing?

Yes, he could be simply showing her his new, second vehicle, because he was a wealthy professional athlete. But she'd been living with him for over a month now and knew that wasn't it. Plus his gigantic grin was a dead giveaway.

"Adjust the seat and mirrors. Program your favorite radio stations."

"No."

People didn't buy her a truck. *Nobody* cared that much. They had an agreement, and this was way beyond its scope.

"Landon..." she said, easing to the edge of the porch, unable to tear her eyes from the vehicle's shiny, perfect beauty. "This is for me, isn't it?"

"Of course!"

"Well, I can't." She crossed her arms. The idea of accepting a gift this expensive sent the breath rushing from her lungs.

"Sure you can."

"No, Landon. This is ridiculous! I won't drive it or accept it. Nick got Alexa's truck going again for me."

"How many times has it died on you in the past week?"

She threw her hands in the air. It wasn't like it had left them on the side of the road. It either started or it didn't. Once it was running, it was fine. Sure, the old Ford wasn't her first choice, but she needed all of her savings for Dusty.

And letting Landon act like her sugar daddy on such a grand scale? It would ruin their whole dynamic. Besides, she'd bet this beauty had every upgrade under the sun, which went way beyond "just solving a problem," like he'd surely claim.

She chucked the key fob back at him.

"The truck isn't about you," Landon said in a hurt, sharp tone.

"You said you had something out here to help me with the kids."

"I do!" He waved toward the vehicle like a game show host revealing a prize.

"Landon. Just…no." She reached for the door to go back inside. "I'm not your…your sugar *thing*."

"My what?"

"A kept woman. I don't know. What's the name for a woman with a sugar daddy?"

He laughed, which angered her.

"It's not funny!"

She'd already become used to the luxurious fridge, the better-quality food he bought, and a fully present man who talked trucks with her son, as well as fronted her interest-free money for her Christmas tree business.

But this? This was too much.

She could save up for her own vehicle. One that wouldn't disappear when he did.

He was still chuckling, and she was ready to pummel his big, wide chest with her fists. Anything to make him stop laughing at her.

He recovered enough to speak. "The truck isn't about you, so get over it, Cass. This is about Rylnn."

"She can't drive."

"Do you know how much I spent on a car service because of my difficult hours, and because I didn't want a live-in nanny?" He'd come up onto the porch and was guiding Cass toward the beautiful truck, a firm, warm hand on her elbow.

"Getting your nanny to and from work wasn't your responsibility."

"When I'd get home after midnight it was. I wasn't going to send a young woman out into the night, relying on public transportation to get her home safely."

"Why didn't you buy *her* a car?"

"I didn't trust her driving. So I paid a crazy bill each month to have someone drive her to and from the condo, as well as take Rylnn to the playground, birthday parties and doctor's appointments."

They'd reached the truck, and he released her. "I could do the same here, if you prefer."

It was a threat. One he knew would work.

Cass snatched the fob from his hand. "What are the strings?"

"Strings?"

"Strings attached? Here's a truck, but…"

"It's a lease. It goes back in three years."

"And? Your expectations for me?" She faced him, arms crossed.

"How do I solve problems, Cass?"

She sighed. "With money."

"What's my job here?"

Right. "Reduce friction."

She felt silly. The truck truly wasn't about her, or them, or anything but him making sure his daughter got where she needed to go, safely. And that Cass had a bit of independence.

"I'm sorry," she said. "There's something seriously wrong with my mind."

She glanced at the door, and Landon opened it

for her. The slightly nauseating scent of New Truck hit her.

"This vehicle," he said, helping her onto the running board and into the soft, light brown leather seat, "is about caring for my daughter. It's about solving what's becoming a reoccurring problem."

He was reaching across Cass, jabbing buttons to adjust her seat, the vents, the steering wheel. His moves were sharp, his eyebrows a sexy line slashing across his forehead.

"You're mad?" she asked.

"I'm frustrated."

"Me, too. So let's get something straight." She smacked his hand away from the controls. "I can take care of myself."

"You shouldn't have to choose between having a reliable vehicle when you live in the boonies, and your son's health. If you're going to continue taking care of my daughter, I need to know that she's safe and not going to be stuck at the side of the road somewhere, like she was on Halloween. I've held off on this as long as I could, Cass."

She sighed, caressing the lovely leather-stitched steering wheel. He wasn't wrong. "I'm vegan. Leather isn't my thing." She tried to slide out of the truck, but he blocked her exit. It was fall into his arms or stay put.

"You're not vegan."

"Landon, this model is too much. You know that, right?"

"You need a truck. Not a car."

"So you bought me the fanciest one you could find in the state of Texas?" One with lighter colors so it wouldn't turn into a sauna in the scorching summer heat. The thing was a masterpiece of engineering beauty.

"If you prefer, I can trade it for a tiny, cheap car that'll barely fit the kids and dog. Maybe not even the dog."

"Don't be a jerk."

He gave her a grin, knowing she'd caved and was going to accept the truck. "I thought I already was."

Cass sighed, pulled up her big girl panties and admitted the truth. "I hate that you had to step in and save me."

"This is just a tool that helps me do my job."

Right. The tool argument again.

"I'm a tool?" She laughed, swiveling in the seat to try to edge out of the truck again, but he placed his hands on her knees, preventing her from moving. The warmth of his hands was distracting, as well as the question of whether they'd slide a little higher.

"Cass, you're like a jigsaw, carving intricate, beautiful patterns into our lives. Before, I was trying to get the job done with a hacksaw."

"Oh." The words hit like a compliment would, but they also made her feel…well, as if none of this was personal. And it should be personal and important, shouldn't it? A *moment*.

They had become more than just two people trying to solve their problems together, hadn't they?

"So you're calling me a tool?" she joked feebly.

"I'm reducing friction." His hands slid to the outside of her thighs as he leaned closer, his expression earnest. "You're part of my home life." He tipped his head toward the lodge. "This is my foundation, remember? Money allows me to buy the tools to ensure that you and my daughter are safe, and you can do your best job. Because when you do, I know Rylnn's taken care of, and then I can put my mental energy into doing my best job at the rink. When I do that, I earn more money." His hands slid off her thighs as though he hadn't even noticed he'd been touching her. "Basically, you've helped me earn the money to buy this truck."

Cass swallowed and dropped to the dirt driveway, wedging herself between his solid body and the truck. "Well, that's some interesting logic. But, uh, thank you. For that."

She stepped away, moving toward the house, the truck's fob clenched in her hand. She paused, turning back. "By the way, it's going to look like crap by the time the lease is over. You're going to lose a lot of money."

His eyes met hers. "It's worth it."

She swallowed over a lump that formed in her throat, wishing her own father had been as invested in her as Landon was in Rylnn. "You're a good dad."

He shrugged. "What's the use of money if you don't spend it?"

"What indeed. But it's going to really suck when you move out and I have to go back to the original Cinderella lifestyle."

The worst part was that Dusty would feel it, too, because no matter how much Cass wished for a fairy godmother, she couldn't turn pumpkins—or Christmas trees—into a new vehicle for them. Not without Landon.

* * *

"Okay, we're here," Landon said, then jumped out of the car and jogged across the wide sidewalk to the arena's will-call ticket booth. Bringing Cass and the kids to a home game had been a last-minute idea, and tickets were waiting for them on the other side of the window.

The window with the Closed sign hanging in it.

Cass, who had bought his "tool" speech last week and accepted the new, fully loaded truck, had also lit up at the idea of watching him play live. The house had suddenly been a whirlwind of energy as they got ready to ride into the city with him.

It felt good.

Everything felt good.

Cass had applied to the Dragons' new sick kids' charity foundation for some financial support with Dusty's medical bills. Her Christmas trees were selling, the kids were happy, Cass was singing Christmas carols nearly every morning, and Landon got to come home every night to an amazing group of people he considered family, as well as wake up in a place that felt like home. Even his ankle was finally healing, impressing the team's physical therapist. And his agent had a few talks lined up with possible sponsors and companies looking to have a sports celebrity in their commercials.

Although he wasn't so sure about the shaving cream ad, where they wanted him to go shirtless. He'd run the idea past Cass and she'd seemed bothered, though all she'd said was, "How will Rylnn feel when she's a teen and sees you posing like that?"

Yeah, yeah. She was right. Objectification. Accepting cash in exchange for prancing around like a sex symbol. He might as well invite a crowd of frenzied fans to come camp out in Sweetheart Creek.

But he'd also heard a hint of possessiveness in Cass's tone. Though that may have simply been wishful thinking.

Landon rapped on the window and cupped his hands around his face, trying to see inside. What was up with the ticket booth? He had a pregame meeting in a few minutes and couldn't just leave Cass and the kids out here without a way inside.

"I thought they gave players free admittance," a sweet voice said from right behind him. Landon cringed, not needing to look in order to know this fan was going to try to touch him, press her body against his. It was all in her tone.

"They're for family," he managed to grind out, keeping his back to the woman.

He spotted a security guard and gave a subtle lift of his chin. The man stepped closer, his stance widening.

Landon turned to face the fan. Her eyes were huge, her words breathy as she slid closer, trying to anchor herself in his personal space while she cooed about his strength and how handsome he was in real life.

He shifted, careful not to get trapped in the lineup corrals behind him.

"Mr. Jackson," the security guard said, his tone all authority, "I can let you in." He gestured toward the tall metal entrance gate to his left.

"I need tickets for my family." Landon flicked his eyes toward his idling car.

"Head through like usual. I'll radio ahead to the gate." The guard seamlessly moved between him and the woman.

"Thanks, Lenny," Landon clapped him on the shoulder, feeling a rush of gratitude. He jogged to the car, trusting that Lenny would direct the woman in the opposite direction.

He didn't need security often, but the few times he had, the man had been present like a guardian angel.

Back in the car, Landon muttered, "Remind me to put him on my Christmas list."

"The security guard?" Cass asked, looking over her shoulder and out the window as Landon drove toward the players' secured back lot. Her hands were in fists, her spine straight as though on alert. "Who was that woman?"

"She likes selfies," Rylnn announced, piping up from the backseat.

"You know her?" Landon's grip tightened on the steering wheel and he jerked the car around the corner, barely containing the sudden surge of rage rippling through him.

"Nanny let her take selfies with us. She always had my favorite cherry bubble gum. She said it was *so* boring waiting outside the apartment and that you were never around."

Landon's vision tilted, and the steering wheel's leather casing creaked in his tight grip.

"Don't take gum or candy from strangers. Ever!" Cass stated firmly, just as Landon snapped, "Never ever take things from strangers, you hear me, Rylnn?"

"Okay," she said quietly, no doubt surprised by both adults' reactions.

"And you don't take selfies with strangers, either," Landon said. "It's called boundaries."

"Okay."

"And don't go anywhere without an adult you know like me or Cass. Even if you've met them before."

"Okay."

As Landon stopped behind another car at the gate, he asked Cass, his voice low, "Have you had to deal with anything like that?" He flicked his gaze toward the backseat.

"No." She shook her head almost fiercely. "Not at all."

"Do you have a shotgun?" He meant it as a joke, but it came out tersely. Tension was radiating to his temples, a sure sign he'd grind his teeth in his sleep tonight and wake in the morning with a headache.

"Of course I do," Cass said with false lightness. "What self-respecting Texan living out in the boonies doesn't?"

The tension began to ease off. His instinct to trust Cass, to add her to their lives, had not been wrong. She would go to the mat for Rylnn if the need should ever arise.

Landon double-checked that he'd locked the doors, feeling as if something more was needed to ensure safe boundaries were in place between his family and grasping fans. He tapped the steering wheel and stared at the car in front of them. Shiny, new and flashy. It had to be Mullens. Landon couldn't keep track of the man's vehicles, which came in and out of his life almost as fast as the women.

Thank goodness Landon had found Cass and Sweetheart Creek. His life was good. Incidents with fans had sharply declined since he'd moved to the country. It was all going to be okay.

Feeling gratitude for his life, and for those who were looking out for him and his daughter, Landon reached over and gave Cass's knee a quick squeeze.

She jumped at his sudden touch.

"Sorry."

"Oh. No, sorry, you took me by surprise," she said breathlessly. "Hey, do you remember that plus-one thing we were discussing?"

"Yeah?" There had never been what he'd call a discussion. The few times he'd suggested the two of them filling in as each other's dates she'd laughed it off.

The security guard laughing, waved Mullens into the back lot.

"It's your turn." Cass pointed to the gate.

Landon rolled forward, letting his window down. The security guard bent to look into the vehicle. "Cruella—sorry, *Nuvella* from PR—will be bringing tickets down for your guests."

"Thank you."

The man nodded, let them through, then closed the gate behind them.

"Sorry, what were you saying?" Landon asked Cass.

They jumped as both kids squealed, "It's Dezzie!"

Sure enough, the Dragons' mascot was padding around the parking lot, dancing to an internal beat. The children were out of the car as soon as it stopped, racing over to give the giant Dragon a hug.

"No running, Dusty!" Cass called after him, then sighed. "I don't think he heard me." She released her seat belt, smiling at the scene. Whatever she'd been about to say about them filling in as each other's dates had obviously been forgotten.

Landon gripped the wheel in frustration. He wanted to hear what she'd been thinking, and wasn't too proud to admit it. He wanted to pursue the subject, hunt it down, ensnare it.

"Violet does such a good job as mascot, doesn't she?" Cass said, reaching for the door.

"What were you going to say?" Landon asked, his tone more impatient than he'd intended.

"What? Oh, nothing. Never mind."

"Tell me."

"The fan just… That was unsettling. I'm not used to it." She flashed a quick smile.

"And so you were going to suggest we date?"

"No," she said quickly. "No. I was just going to say that if it helps you out, you can tell your fans that… Well, you could give them the impression that we, you know…"

"Impression that we what?" He needed to hear her say it.

"You know, just if it helps you out. People around town already assume we're dating, so maybe it would help if your rabid fangirls thought the same thing."

She wouldn't look at him, was fidgeting, sucking in her cheeks.

If he didn't know better, he'd think Cassandra McTavish had a crush on him.

He pushed what was likely an overoptimistic thought from his mind and forced himself to be logical about fake-dating his friend and nanny.

"What about the kids?" he asked, working hard to sound casual. "Didn't you say that ending our agreement would feel like a divorce? Wouldn't this make it worse?"

"Keeping you and Rylnn safe is the most important thing right now," Cass stated, turning to him. Her hazel eyes drilled into him with determination.

Landon gazed back at her, feeling a sting of pride that she was wearing one of his old jerseys tonight. He liked that. More than he'd ever admit to anyone.

"We can worry about the future when we get there," she said, her tone all business, even though her cheeks were becoming flushed.

"Right."

"You're family, Landon." That single-minded expression was back, the same don't-argue-with-me look she gave the kids. "We watch out for each other. This would just be another tool in our toolbox."

"You calling me a tool?" he joked.

She pursed her lips, and he wasn't sure if she was embarrassed or trying to convince herself of her words. "Neither of us is looking for something deep or meaningful. This isn't a connection that'll last through all time and eternity." There was a wryness to her tone, as if she was mocking the idea of true love and soul mates.

It made him want to pummel her ex. And not for the first time.

* * *

Landon wasn't replying to Cass's proposal, and she was freaking out inside. She'd really put herself out there, and his lack of response was embarrassing.

Maybe he was worried she'd misinterpret his need for the occasional date as meaning something more. Because a gala's plus-one, versus letting everyone think you were dating, was not the same thing.

What if he thought she was being possessive and jealous?

She did feel possessive, but mostly protective. Moments ago, she'd wanted to march out of the car and rip that woman's throat out. She wanted to be a firm barrier between Landon and Rylnn and the outside world. Their private lives were precious, and whatever she could do to protect that, she would.

Rylnn and Landon were part of her family now, and she was determined to look out for them just like Landon looked out for her and Dusty.

Sure, it could hurt the kids if they believed the relationship was real, and then she and Landon went their separate ways. But right now she believed the good outweighed the bad with ratcheting up their relationship into something fake.

"So, yeah. Crazy idea, right?" she said, into the ongoing silence.

Outside the car, Dusty and Rylnn were playing with Violet, dressed up in her plush mascot costume. Fearing Landon thought she was actually one of his fangirl crazies in disguise, Cass got out when he continued to sit silently, hands grasping the steering wheel. She joined the kids and the mascot and snapped a few photos with her phone.

One of the players, a beefy man with a hint of tattoos peeking above his shirt collar and tie, had exited his sports car, and came over to stand beside Cass. "Want a photo with Dezzie?" he asked, gesturing to the kids and the dragon.

Landon appeared at Cass's side. "We're fine, Mullens."

Cass frowned at the strange edge in his voice.

Mullens shrugged easily and turned away.

"Actually," Cass called, shooting Landon a chiding look for being so curt, "we'd love one."

The man returned, giving her a charming

smile that lit up his long-lashed eyes. He was handsome and had a way of gazing at a person that made them feel noticed. She was pretty sure he probably looked at every woman the way he was at her, but it didn't lessen the impact.

"I'm Cass," she said, offering her hand.

He grasped it with both of his huge ones, giving it a warm shake, and she could feel her cheeks turning pink at the attention.

"Mullens, this is my girlfriend, Cassandra Mc-Tavish," Landon said tightly. "You can call her Cassandra."

Cass flashed Landon a questioning look. Girlfriend? Did that mean he was agreeing to the fake-dating thing?

"Is that what the jersey's about?" Mullens asked, his tone teasing as he glanced at Cass's shirt. One hand moved to her elbow, gently cupping it and sending shivers up her arm.

She'd never met anyone like him before. The hockey player was definitely in her personal space, but for whatever reason, she didn't mind. He probably had women age eighteen to seventy-three swooning in his wake.

"I play with The Blockade," he said, gesturing toward Landon without sparing him a glance. "Number 16."

"You can let go of her now," Landon said, shoving his phone at Mullens.

"Just letting her know how to find me on the ice."

Landon pulled Cass over to Dezzie, where he lined them up with the kids in front of the mascot. "Hey, Vi."

Inside the costume, the woman turned, holding up her giant dragon hands as though confused as to who this "Vi" was.

"Sorry, I mean Dezzie."

The big plush mascot gave him a hug, and Cass laughed. She wasn't sure how Landon was going to play tonight, as it appeared every emotion was winding its way through him.

Seriously, had he been jealous of Mullens? Yeah, sure, she could see it. Mullens had an effect. But it wasn't real. Or deep. He was nothing like Landon.

Still, she couldn't help but wonder if jealousy or possessiveness had spurred him to say yes to a fake relationship deal.

Mullens took their photo, and then the six of them filtered into the arena, where Mullens and Dezzie went their separate ways. Landon hung back, and Cass asked quickly, "So, are we fake dating?"

Landon's eyes immediately flicked in the direction Mullens had disappeared. He gave a tight nod. "Still works for you?"

"I suggested it," she said lightly.

Landon's gaze met hers before dropping.

"This won't make things weird, will it?" she asked.

The tension vanished as he looked up. "No."

"Good."

A woman was hustling toward them on bright red stilettos, her hair short and bleached within an inch of its life. "I have your tickets, Jackson. Plan ahead next time."

Cass rolled up onto her tiptoes, planting a kiss on Landon's cheek. "Have a good game."

Then, proudly wearing his jersey, she accepted the tickets, gathered the kids and followed the signs that led to where they would sit and watch her new fake boyfriend play.

Because even though he hadn't chosen her for romantic reasons, like her ex-husband had, for some reason it felt even better.

CHAPTER 9

$\mathcal{C}$ass watched Landon navigate around her kitchen. He was comfortable, competent, and moved with efficiency as he chopped onions, tossing them into a pan of sizzling butter. Just like he was on the ice, protecting the team's net.

The kitchen smelled amazing. When Alexa and Cash came over that evening for their early Thanksgiving feast, they were going to be blown away, if the scents were anything to go by.

Since Landon had an out-of-town game on Thanksgiving Day, Cass had suggested they have a meal earlier in the week, on Sunday instead of Thursday. And because he had the day off, Landon had offered to take care of the food. She had to admit that having him around was a hundred times better than she could have imagined. Not only had he arranged for her and the kids to sit down near the ice during his game—sadly, the Dragons hadn't won despite his amazing saves—he was helping out with all sorts of things. Some days it was hard to believe their arrangement was truly real.

"Men who cook are pretty sexy, you know," Cass said, taking a sip of the chocolate-peppermint latte he'd made with the hissing, shiny machine that had appeared on her counter last week. It was like drinking heaven. All chocolatey and fresh.

He hadn't shaved yet this morning, and she had to say that her fake-boyfriend looked as sexy as a real one. Not that they were doing that. In fact, since the game a few weeks ago, there'd been no reason to pull out the "he's my boyfriend" card. It had all been very anticlimactic, with them slipping right back into their old life again.

Which was good.

She didn't need him presenting her to everyone like a girlfriend to feel decent about herself.

Although she understood the appeal of having a sexy man like him with a bit of pro sports status claiming her as his choice. That would be pretty hot.

"Cass, careful now," he teased lightly. "Calling me sexy might make me think you're hitting on me."

"I'm a big catfish honeybee."

She scooped up the gray-and-white kitten that kept sneaking into the house, putting it out onto the back porch, where PC gave it a giant lick upside the head in welcome, nearly knocking it off its feet.

"Um, you're a what?" Landon's face scrunched adorably.

"You know. Out trying to trick people into loving me."

"Oh!" His eyes lit up with comprehension. "I think you mean honeypot? Or cat fishing?"

She shrugged. "Whatever. You know what I mean."

"Do I, though? We're platonic, Cass." His brows had lifted, and he was giving her a sexy, you'd-best-behave sort of look that sent tingles through her body. "I might add that I've noticed you put your hands all over me whenever you get a chance."

She laughed. They barely touched. Sure, she would gently lay a hand on his waist when he was staring into the fridge, trying to sort out what he was allowed to eat that day, and she needed to reach around him. And she might brush dog hair or crumbs off his suit shirts any chance she got. But still. She was just preventing kitchen collisions, as well as ensuring he didn't get photographed coming off a plane looking unkempt.

"It's those hunky quads," she said, not kidding, but trying to make it sound as though she was. "Irresistible."

He chuckled and moved one pan from the heat. "I'll be sure to remember that next time Karlene, the team's physical therapist, is killing me on the stationary bike."

"How's your ankle? You never talk about it."

Landon shifted his weight as though testing it. "Pretty much healed."

"Good." She'd noticed it was stiff sometimes, but when she watched his games on TV, he was up and down, on and off his knees as if he'd never had ankle issues. Then he'd come home, no sign of a limp other than the odd night when he'd had to twist too far to the right to make a save.

He dumped the pan's contents into a bowl. "It's good. And I'm getting noticed."

"By your fangirls." Since the team had won a few games, he was being recognized more by the media.

More airtime in postgame wrap-ups, shots of him leaving the arena and signing autographs for young women. Younger than Cass, anyway. He wasn't quite as popular as Mullens, the team forward, or the center, Dylan. Although Dylan was usually scowling at the camera like the photographer had repeatedly stepped on his toes or something.

"I meant sponsors."

"Any in particular?" She came closer, rubbing the stubble on his chin, hinting at the still-open offer from a shaving company.

"You suggesting I should shave before your sister comes over?"

"Yeah. She has a thing for five o'clock shadow."

Landon looked alarmed.

"I'm kidding." He'd be good in a shaving commercial, though. Any man would want to look like him. All angles and handsome solemnness when he was concentrating on something. Although they wanted him shirtless. Who didn't, though? Cass had seen him without a shirt and it was a stunning look on him.

She did worry, though, that him strutting about like a sex symbol would make his popularity skyrocket and she'd actually have to make use of that shotgun she'd joked about. Would his fans find the way out to Sweetheart Creek and make their lives chaotic? Cass wasn't sure, but didn't really want to risk it.

"Pass me the chopped apple?" Landon asked from his spot at the stove. Earlier, she'd jokingly tossed him a ruffled apron that had been her mother's, and he'd put it on without a second thought. It was cute. Really cute. A big, tough hockey player with low-slung jeans over tight muscles and wide shoulders that were strong enough to carry her—he'd proved that during a pillow fight with the kids, where he'd tossed her over his shoulder to help her escape the onslaught—and wearing something frilly turned her crank.

Her crank should not be turning. It had been decommissioned a long time ago, and it had absolutely no business being recommissioned right now. Or ever.

Sure, she loved that Landon continually distracted her from the stress of having so many unanswered questions surrounding Dusty. If it weren't for Landon she'd be a ball of nerves, trying to intuit whether it was best for the surgery to happen now or when he was older. But seriously...her crank really needed to shut itself down.

"You need to shave," she said, distracting herself by sweeping up a bit of onion skin from between two bowls.

"It's okay, I'll get it." Landon moved a few steps, reaching across her to grab his prepped apple, his arm brushing hers and sending tingles up it.

"Apple? For your stuffing?"

"Where did you think it was going?" He dumped it into a pan.

"A pie, obviously."

"You're making the pies."

"I thought you were being extra sweet and helpful, like always. You know, taking on all my cooking duties."

"No way. You need to put a finger in every pot today. It's your family coming over, so if anything goes wrong, it falls squarely on your shoulders."

"Don't forget about Nick and Polly."

"As I said, your family."

Cass laughed. "They just work on Alexa's ranch."

"Family are the people you choose."

"True." She snuck a bit closer to Landon, stole

a chunk of apple from his pan and popped it in her mouth. "Oh, hot!"

He gave her a look and shook his head.

She held a hand over her open mouth and breathed past the steaming bite, trying to cool it. "What? I didn't expect it to be so hot already."

Truthfully, she was tickled to be hosting. She felt like a woman who had her feet under her for the first time in a long while.

Last year, she'd been already engrossed in the long Montana winter, and had only thrown something quick together for the ranch hands. Today her table would be filled with people who cared about her and weren't just there for the free meal. It was a good feeling.

Landon dumped some spices in with the apple, filling the room with fresh smells.

"Where did you learn to cook?" she asked him.

"My grandma."

In early October, Landon and Rylnn had flown to Canada for Canadian Thanksgiving and had seen his family. Cass hadn't even realized the two countries held Thanksgiving at different times of the year.

"Can you read out the temperatures and times for me again?" he asked, taking the turkey out of the fridge and setting it on the kitchen island.

Leaning her butt against the counter, Cass picked up the faded and stained scrap of paper with Landon's grandma's recipe for turkey and stuffing. "Four hundred for the first thirty minutes."

He stepped briskly into her space, reaching for something on the shelf above her. She started to move left to give him more room, but he placed a hand on her hip, holding her there.

"You're fine. Keep reading."

His thighs pressed against hers as he stretched to reach the top shelf, pushing the recipe she held against her chest.

"Why don't you let me move?" she laughed. His eyes drifted from his task down to hers. The hand on her hip suddenly felt so much warmer, the heat going deep.

"You know," she said, lowering her voice, "maybe this is why people assume we're dating. You're always in my personal space."

He didn't step back as he set the large metal mixing bowl on the counter at her side. "Does that bother you? I thought that was the point?"

She didn't mention that there was nobody else in the kitchen to witness them, and thus no need to act. But she shrugged, feeling the heat rise within her. "I could do worse."

People thinking she was dating an NHL goalie wasn't exactly a hardship. Especially when he was so amazing with the kids, and was naturally kind, thoughtful and generous.

She hoped he never found a reason to go live in his own place again.

He chuckled, his eyes crinkling. "Good. Because, Cass—" he gently stroked a finger under her chin "—sometimes we need people in our space."

* * *

"Cass!" Landon called from his spot at the stove. Alexa and Cash would be over in an hour and a half for Thanksgiving and it was crunch time with the meal prep. "Cass! Your phone's ringing."

He took a few steps, a loose tile underfoot chirping at him as he reached for her phone, checking caller ID to see if it was important. Dusty's cardiologist. "Cass!"

If she didn't catch this call, she could be playing phone tag for the rest of the week as they bumped up against the actual Thanksgiving holiday.

He wasn't going to let that happen. She'd been waiting too long to talk to the surgeon. Landon had seen the shadowed look in her eyes from time to time since Halloween. He'd noticed the way she'd catch herself tensing and force her shoulders down, along with a deep breath into her lungs.

He answered the call as he turned down the stove's burners. "Hello?"

"Is Cassandra there, please." The doctor's voice was smooth and reassuring.

"Just a moment. I'll find her." Landon maneuvered out of the kitchen, finding the kids in the midst of some sort of performance on the fireplace's thick stone hearth. "Have you seen Cass?"

"Wanna see our play?" Rylnn asked.

"It's about pilgrims," Dusty said, sitting cross-legged in front of her. He had a flashlight, a basket of plastic toy snakes, and what looked like confetti. Landon didn't want to ask.

"When I'm done cooking, I definitely do." He continued on through the house, following the sound of banging. He took the stairs up, then turned down a narrow hallway that led to the large room that overlooked the backyard. His eyebrows lifted in surprise. Cass had been busy. The couple-hundred-square-foot space no longer had carpet, and the old wood floors were exposed. The planking had seen better days, but he'd witnessed what Cass could do with something used and worn. In other words, the former smoking room would soon look rustic, charming and welcoming.

"Cass? It's for you." He held out her phone and mouthed *"Doctor."*

Her grip on the crowbar went slack, the tool falling onto a bundle of shredded carpet. Her cowboy boots clomped across the floor and she answered her phone with a breathless "Hello?"

Landon eased toward the door, then paused, one hand on the jamb. He glanced at Cass, who had moved to the large, dusty windows, her shoulders tense.

"Yes, I can do that. Just me?" She looked over at him, her eyes wide with immediate concern. "I understand. Yes, of course. Not a problem. See you then."

With a shaky exhale, she slid the phone into the back pocket of her Wranglers.

"Everything all right?"

"She wants to see me later this week." Cass picked up the crowbar and for a second Landon wasn't sure if she wanted to throw it or let it drop back onto the carpet.

"Just you?" he asked, alarm trickling its way up his spine.

"No Dusty," she confirmed. "She wants to talk specifics."

Landon's blood ran cold. "What does that mean?"

"She wants to run more in-depth tests at the hospital to rule out some abnormalities in Dusty's results. She needs to keep him for a few days. Then we'll discuss what kind of surgery." Her voice wavered.

"Heart surgery?" he whispered. "It's for sure now?"

She gave a small nod.

"When?"

She cleared her throat, her expression stricken. "Around Christmas."

Landon pulled her into his arms, not quite sure when he'd made his way across the room. As far as he knew, she was keeping Dusty mostly in the dark about his condition—whatever it ended up being. But soon she'd have to tell him, prep him for hospital stays, more tests, then surgery and recovery.

"I don't know if I can do this," she said, her voice muffled against his shoulder.

"You can."

She was hugging him, her arms hooked along

his sides, her hands gripping his shoulders with surprising strength.

"I'm here, Cass. You can do this. I'll help."

She pushed out of his arms, looking at him as though she didn't quite trust his words.

"Do you want me to go with you? To the appointment?"

"I'm sure you have a game, or a practice." She was trying to back away, but he held fast.

"We have a backup goalie for a reason."

"I couldn't ask you to miss work."

"You don't have to. What time do we need to be there? Can Alexa watch the kids?"

"I don't know."

"Do you want me to ask? And then ask Hannah as backup?"

Cass was nodding slowly, strength seeming to seep back into her bones, and Landon let out a sigh of relief. Seeing someone so strong have moments of doubt was disconcerting.

He gave her arms a squeeze. "I'm serious about this. I'm here. Absolutely anytime you need me."

"I'm just a tool," she said, with a shake of her head.

It took him a moment to realize she was referring to how he'd defined her place in his life: as a tool to help him achieve the things he wanted to. He felt like a jerk for ever having said that.

"You're more than a tool. You're my family, my friend. And you're more important than anything that could ever happen at the rink."

With shock, he realized that was true.

* * *

"You didn't tell me he cooks, too," Cass's sister murmured as she came to a halt in the kitchen doorway.

Landon turned from where he was pulling the turkey out of the oven. "What can I say? I'm the complete package."

"Real men cook!" Dusty said, popping up from behind the counter and receiving a high five from Landon.

"Oh! I didn't see you there, little man." Alexa frowned at the frilly apron wrapped around Dusty's tiny frame. "What have you got on?" She turned to Cass. "Is that Mom's?"

She nodded.

"Landon and I were whipping the cream for pie!" Dusty said. "I got to lick the beaters."

"I took a million pictures. It was so cute." Cass had done some major swooning as Landon patiently taught her son things she'd never considered doing. How on earth did she plan to raise a man who helped out around the house if she didn't teach him? She was still shaking her head at herself for that oversight.

Then again, Dusty was only five. He helped set the table and such, but she hadn't thought of him doing much more.

Alexa was looking at her, eyebrows raised, with a knowing, slightly taunting smile. Cass scowled at her and then schooled her own expression. She didn't need her sister thinking and acting like she was crushing on Landon—even though most people thought they were already the real deal.

Landon tugged at the apron strings, freeing Dusty with a few swoops of fabric. "Your civic duty is complete."

"What?"

"You're free to go play. Thanks for your help." Landon dropped the apron over his own neck and turned back to the stove.

Dusty zipped off, more energetic than Cass had seen him in days. It filled her heart with hope, especially after the surgeon's concerning call. "Landon's been amazing with Dusty," she said, realizing she was gushing.

Alexa studied Landon from head to toe, her eyes narrowing as she took him in. "Obviously, you must leave dirty laundry everywhere or something, because no man is perfect."

Her husband came up behind her, slid his hands around her waist and hugged her close. "What about me?" Cash placed a noisy kiss on the nape of her neck. "Aren't I perfect?"

"Kisses like this are supposed to be sensual." Alexa tapped her neck and Cash complied, performing a do-over. He pressed a lingering kiss on a spot beneath her jaw that made Alexa bite her lower lip, then turn and sling her arms around him.

Cass rolled her eyes, smirking at Landon as though to say *Can you believe these two?* They'd been together long enough to be out of the honeymoon phase. Still, Cass couldn't help but wish with a touch of envy that she could have some snuggles like that in her own life. Her ex had never been what she considered cuddly, and she couldn't quite imagine putting on a public display like her sister often did with Cash.

"Does that make up for leaving laundry everywhere?" Cash asked.

"Mmm. I'll think on it," Alexa said with a devilish glint in her eye. She turned to Landon. "Do you give neck kisses like that?"

"I do laundry." He pointedly kept his attention on the turkey.

"He does," Cass agreed, wishing she could answer the kissing question from her own very personal knowledge base.

Alexa ran a hand down the shiny fridge to her right. She said to Cash, "He also buys amazing appliances. It makes ice."

"I make ice," Cash replied. "And you told me you don't care about money. You care about me."

She gave a sweet smile that had Cash frowning. "What can I help with?" he asked Landon.

"You could open the wine. It's in the fridge."

Alexa perked up, pulling a bottle from her shoulder bag and setting it on the counter. "We brought wine. Even though I prefer Budweiser." She winked at her husband and dug out her pocketknife, ever-present in her Wranglers, then sliced through the foil, despite the pull tab. Cass got out glasses.

"Corkscrew?" Alexa asked.

Cash rifled through the kitchen drawers, before tossing her one.

"You didn't buy a bottle with a twist-off cap?" Cass teased.

"No, no. NHLers deserve wine with corks," her sister said with authority.

"Thanks for thinking of me, but I'm actually off the sauce," Landon said apologetically. "During the season Athena has us on a pretty strict diet. No alcohol."

"We could have bought the cheap stuff?" Cash said remorsefully.

Alexa elbowed him, then glanced at Cass. "Athena's Hannah's cousin, and lives around here, right?"

Alexa had moved to Texas a few years before Cass did and between the two of them they were putting together a mental who's-who of the Sweetheart Creek community.

She nodded. It seemed like everyone around here either knew or was related to everyone else. It was a lot like Montana in that sense, and sometimes it made her miss home, though that feeling seemed to have waned a lot in recent weeks.

* * *

As Landon continued working on the meal, the two sisters caught up on the latest gossip. Some of which included Athena Gavras, the team's dietician, opening a store with her own sister in downtown Sweetheart Creek.

"A dietician store?" Landon asked, feeling confused.

"Coffee, books and little knickknacks."

"Cool." He hoped that didn't mean she was quitting the team.

"Oh, I forgot." Alexa clamped a hand over her mouth. "We kind of also invited Jenny Oliver today."

"No problem," Landon said. "There's plenty to go around."

"Landon," Cass said, "hide your credit card."

"Why's that?"

"Jenny owns Blue Tumbleweed and Rylnn's got her eye on some baby blue cowboy boots."

Landon smiled. Cass was turning his daughter into a true-blue cowgirl. He had a feeling Cass enjoyed buying cute things for his daughter on his card. She never asked for anything for herself or for Dusty, and never went overboard or had Dusty feeling left out, but her taste was exquisite and suited Rylnn to a T.

"Perfect," he said, wishing there was a way he could buy boots for Dusty and Cass as well, without her turning him down.

"Remember those white cowboy boots you got as a kid?" Alexa asked her sister.

Cass groaned. "I let my inner diva shine just once…" she said, before Alexa began to relay how Cass had begged and begged for a pair of white cowboy boots when she was eight.

"They had rainbow-threaded designs," she explained. It was clear that eight-year-old Cass had never seen anything more beautiful.

"They were expensive," Alexa stated.

"I chipped in the extra twenty bucks!"

"Anyway, she somehow convinced Mom to get them for her, but then refused to wear them outside." Alexa hooted.

Cass's cheeks turned an endearing pink as she argued, "They'd get dirty!"

"Cowboy boots are *meant* for chores."

"Not those ones!"

"So by the second day Mom and Dad were so frustrated with Cass refusing to do chores in what were now her only boots that Dad picked her up and carried her out to the barn. He dropped her in her boots right in the dirt and straw."

Landon saw a flicker of hurt settle in Cass's eyes.

"Cass started crying and taking off her boots in the middle of the muck."

"They were getting dirty!"

"It's a miracle she became a rancher at all."

So Cass did indeed have an inner princess. Interesting. She kept that side of herself well-hidden. Although maybe it was one of the reasons she and Rylnn connected. And yet Ry hadn't connected with the princessy nanny. There truly was something special about Cass, wasn't there?

"Mom returned the boots," Cass explained. "She got me the ugliest navy blue ones in exchange." She made dramatic choking sounds, causing Landon to chuckle. "I hated every minute of wearing them."

"Drama much?" Alexa asked drily.

Cass stuck out her tongue and Cash and Landon laughed at the sisters.

Landon drained the cooked potatoes and Cass came over to mash them.

"Nick and Polly are still coming, right?" Landon asked Alexa, referring to her ranch hand and his girlfriend.

"They should be here in a bit."

"I thought Jenny was going over to Maverick's on Friday for a late Thanksgiving?" Cass asked Alexa.

"She is, but I think she's kind of lonely. I remember being single in South Carolina, and sometimes being alone around the holidays just sucked."

"But you had me," Cass protested.

Her sister scrunched her nose and shrugged.

"Hey!" Cass gave her a light push that didn't move her.

"Wait," Landon said. "When did you guys live in South Carolina?"

"You are so *not* Texan," Alexa said. "You need to say 'y'all' if you're going to live around here."

Landon waved the oven mitts in the air and rolled his eyes. "Fine, Miss Montana. I'll start when you do."

"Hey! That's *my* pet name for her. Don't infringe," Cash said.

Landon winced. "Sorry. Anyway, as I was saying—" he began speaking in a slow, drawn-out drawl "—when did y'all live in South Carolina?"

"Well, that's where Dusty was born," Alexa said.

"But I thought *y'all* shared a ranch in Montana?"

"Yeah, but Cass went and fell in love, and moved to South Carolina with Fart Face."

"Hey," Cash warned, glancing around for the kids. "Language."

"I could call him something worse. That's the censored version."

"Yeah, well, I don't think the little man—" he angled his head in the direction Dusty had gone "—needs to hear you slandering his father."

Alexa's face turned red. "You think that's slander?" Her hands were on her hips and she seemed ready to spout off.

Landon stole a glance at Cass. Her face was stoically blank.

"Where is Mr. Fart Face Numb Nuts now? Cass has tried calling hundreds of times. He knows he's needed."

"It's fine," Cass said quickly, darting a glance Landon's way. "It wasn't a hundred, and he's…" She shrugged, as though out of excuses for her ex, or maybe she'd finally reached the stage where she simply didn't want to provide any. The man had made his choices, and it looked like Cass wasn't willing to cover for him.

Landon admired her all the more.

"I'm not sure why I ever believed Archer was The One," Cass said quietly to Landon, her hard tone summing up the situation more than a million stories could.

"Cass had a difficult pregnancy," Alexa was explaining, probably for his benefit, "so I left our guys in charge of the ranch for a bit...."

Cass's eyes fluttered closed. Landon wanted to change the subject, spare her the painful recollections, but he was also curious. Way too curious about her and her past love and what had gone so wrong that the man didn't seem to be a part of things. Even with an ailing son.

"Where are your parents?" Landon asked.

"They've both passed," Cass said.

"Oh, I'm sorry to hear that."

"It's been years." And yet his expression of sympathy dampened her eyes. It may have been a while, but it still held a strong effect on her.

"Anyway," Alexa said, charging along, "I went down to help her, since Numb Nuts was useless."

Cass sighed deeply.

"Then she had a difficult delivery. Dusty was colicky, and then Fart Face decided to divorce Cass and drew it all out for a long time. Disappeared. Didn't pay for support. And so here we are. And he's still useless." She turned to Cash. "Verdict stands. Once a Fart Face always a Fart Face."

"And we've also made the point that I suck at love. Thank you, Alexa."

"Cass," Alexa gave her sister a look of such sympathy and sisterly devotion it made Landon miss his own family. "I love you. You're my sister and I would do anything for you. Just say the word."

She laughed, the pained expression fading away. "I love you, too." She pulled Alexa into a tight hug. "But your indignation is exhausting. You make me feel like a stupid victim every time you tell that story."

"I'm so sorry. I'll stop." She held Cass at arm's length and gave her a leveling look. "But I *will* shoot him if he ever hurts you again."

Hear, hear.

The two sisters separated and Cash reached out, giving Cass's shoulder a squeeze while whispering, "Don't worry, I have bail money tucked away just in case." He winked conspiratorially.

"Hey!" Alexa said, giving him a playful shove.

The three of them laughed, and Landon felt better knowing Cass had someone so fiercely on her side.

He held out a tray of appetizers. "Cheese bite?"

"Don't mind if I do," Cash said, popping one into his mouth.

Cass, shaking her head but smiling, skirted

the kitchen island on her way to the stove to help Landon. She began scooping stuffing from the turkey while he held the pan.

"What's a holiday without a little drama?" he whispered, lightly pressing his shoulder against hers.

She gave a hollow chuckle. "Can you believe I moved across how many states to be closer to her?"

Landon smirked.

"The reason Castor Oil moved was that she couldn't find any suitable men living out in the boonies," Alexa teased.

"Castor Oil?" Landon grimaced at the awful nickname as Cass shot Alexa a glare over her shoulder. "Sisters really *are* the worst."

"Tell me about it," she muttered back.

"Hey," Alexa said, "all I'm saying is that it looks like it worked out with her moving south. Wouldn't you say so, Landon?"

Cass gave him an apologetic look, but he smiled. "Yeah, I'd say it worked out quite well."

CHAPTER 10

Landon jiggled a leg, unable to help himself as Dusty's pediatric cardiologist explained the tests she wanted to run and why. Landon wasn't sure how much Cass was picking up, as his own head was a roar of static and he wasn't even the parent. But she was nodding and making small sounds to show she was following.

Maybe because she'd been eased into this whole thing, the diagnosis getting worse and worse, her tolerance had grown alongside, keeping pace?

But he hadn't experienced that, and the things they wanted to do to Dusty's heart were mind-blowing. The cardiologist figured the boy's heart had grown incorrectly, a vein where an artery was supposed to be, or vice versa. Whatever it was, Landon gathered that something was in the wrong place, but they could fix it.

They could literately reconstruct a heart in a living being. It blew Landon's mind.

The doctor spoke like it was no big deal, but Landon had felt the room tilt when she'd mentioned cracking Dusty's ribs so they could access his small heart.

This felt like a television medical drama. Not real life. Not going to happen to the little boy who cuddled against his side when he read him truck stories.

Landon needed to do something. He needed to call up Dak Morisette, who was working on the Dragons' charity for sick kids, and tell the man he was on board. Originally, he'd said no—it would look like he was way too involved in Cass's life if he volunteered for the very charity she'd be leaning on. It would look as though he'd found a new way to pay for her medical bills, which might spook her or something. It would be too much, too soon. It would look *personal*.

But now? Nothing could be too personal.

He'd volunteer for whatever the charity

needed. Anything. Everything. If they wanted him going door to door and shaking a can for donations, he would. Sell a kidney? He was in. The price couldn't be too high.

* * *

Cass felt like she might pass out. The surgeon kept talking, on and on. So many details, so many complicated terms and procedures. She'd spent enough time surfing the medical channel to know how invasive all this would be.

She wanted to leave. Go. Pretend none of this was happening to her or to her perfect, lovely son.

Except he wasn't perfect. Her difficult pregnancy had created a faulty heart.

She exhaled slowly, trying to dispel the swirling sensation in her head. Everything felt too bright, too...present and loud.

Landon moved in her periphery, leaning forward in his chair, swiping a hand across his cheek as though dashing away a tear.

She blinked and stared unseeing at the doctor, blocking Landon out.

Her little boy. They were going to pause his

heart. They were going to do things that, technically…

No. Don't think about it. Positive thoughts only.

They were going to open him up. Look at his heart. Expose it. Cut it.

She sucked in a deep breath, the room spinning, her stomach clenching.

The surgeon pressed several printouts into her hands. "You understand, Cassandra?"

She nodded mutely.

Then she was standing. The doctor was ushering them toward the door.

The air felt thick, stale, sticking in her throat.

She squeezed her fingers around the list of tests, the quote for her insurance company.

Pages. Pages of numbers, and one giant figure underlined and bolded at the bottom of the last page.

Day one. Admit Dusty to the hospital for more tests to ensure the accuracy of the diagnosis.

Day two. More tests to ensure he was strong enough for one big surgery rather than several small ones.

Day three. Tests that would advise the surgical team's methodology.

Three days. Then home. Then back again for the operation.

She stopped in the doorway. She didn't want to step outside the office without an iron-clad guarantee that this would work. That Dusty would be strong enough to soar through it, that his health wouldn't suddenly plummet.

"Can we get him in this week?" she asked.

"As soon as we can, Cassandra. I understand your urgency. We feel it, too."

Landon's hand was on her elbow, giving a re-assuring squeeze, his chest against her back like a wall. She wished his hockey nickname, The Blockade, would apply to everything in life. That he could somehow shield her from this.

He ushered her forward, and they were suddenly back in the miniature world of the waiting room, filled with child-size furniture and bright murals painted low on the walls. She felt out of place, gigantic. Nothing felt right.

Her head swam, and her jacket, which had warmed her in the office as she warded off a chill, suddenly felt too hot. She pulled at the collar of her shirt and kept moving, focusing on her breath.

Get to the car.

Get home.

Get to Dusty.

"Are you okay?" Landon's hand moved from her elbow to rub gentle circles on her back.

"I can't do this." She stopped moving and his body came up against hers. The hand that had been on her back slid around her shoulder, pulling her to him. She tucked her face against his warm, solid neck, inhaling the familiar scent of him. She didn't care that anyone in the waiting room could see her breaking down, that she might be inflaming someone else's fears.

What was she going to tell Dusty? What was she going to tell her friends?

What if Dusty didn't pull through? What if it was too late? What if this didn't work?

"I can't do this." Panic swirled up within her, consuming her like a rogue wave. She gulped air. "I can't do this. I can't. I can't."

Light-headedness overtook her, and she tried to lean into Landon, but he grabbed her by the shoulders, forcing her to stand on her own feet. His hands framed her face. "Cass, look at me."

She shut her eyes, fighting off the shaky feeling of collapse. She never asked for anything. She just needed him to hold her. Make her strong again.

"Cass," he said firmly. "Look at me."

Unable to ignore the command, she obeyed. His gray eyes were drilling into her with determination and strength.

"Breathe with me. In," he coached. "Out."

Cass complied, breathing with him. His hands moved back to her shoulders, holding her loosely, his eyes still on hers. Gently, he rocked them from side to side. It was like they were dancing, their bodies in sync, and slowly, she fell into the hypnotic comfort of his solid, steady presence.

It reminded her of those long nights when Dusty had been a colicky baby, and Archer was trying to sleep, grumpy at the work-night disturbance. She would walk and rock. Walk and rock. Attempting to transfer her own calm and peace to Dusty, helping him regulate.

"You're a good dad," she told Landon.

She folded herself into his arms, and he held her close. She knew that he'd let her stay here for as long as she needed, and that his hug would be the right pressure, the right everything. Because that was who Landon was.

"And you're a good mom, Cass," he said, stroking her hair.

She sniffed, wishing that was true, that she could go back in time and somehow fix her pregnancy, fix her baby.

"You're not alone," Landon murmured, still rocking them from side to side. "We're going to take care of this one step at a time. Dusty's strong. It's going to work, and you'd better believe I researched this lady."

When Cass looked up at him, he tipped his head toward the office they'd just left. "She's the best in the state, and the Dragons' charity will help with the cost. You have money saved. I have money saved. We've got this."

"You can't—"

"I can. Money is for spending."

"It's a *lot*."

"Then I guess you'll just have to be a nanny for Rylnn a lot longer than you'd planned." The skin around his eyes crinkled, and the anxiety swamping her began to lessen.

Landon wouldn't let her look away. "This, right now, with all the unknowns, is the scariest, darkest moment. If we can make it through this, the rest will be easier."

She bit her lip and nodded, trying to be strong, trying to trust his words.

"We should probably go?" Landon said gently, and Cass drew in a deep breath, feeling dazed as she took in their surroundings and the few waiting parents shooting her worried looks.

One foot in front of the other. Everything was going to be okay. And it was going to be okay because she had Landon.

That alone should have terrified her, because she knew he wasn't forever. But for whatever reason, in this moment, having him in her life simply felt right.

CHAPTER 11

_L_andon scanned the excited crowd of children in the long room in the Cho Memorial Children's Hospital, tension building in his muscles until he spotted Dusty. The boy caught his eye with a gigantic smile and Landon relaxed.

Dusty waved exuberantly. The kids were all pretty excited to have hockey stars come visit, play and read to them, as part of the Dragons' Children's Charity. But by the looks of it, Dusty was the most excited by far.

Landon smiled and waved back, giving the boy a nod.

"I know him! He lives with me and my mom!" Dusty said to the kid next to him.

The room, despite having the sterile feel of all medical buildings, was decked out for the upcoming holidays. There was a small, fake Christmas tree in the corner, some of the staff and volunteers wore Santa hats, and decorations lined the walls. Cass, a big fan of the holiday, would love it here.

Dak, a former NHL player now in charge of the charity, was already giving orders on how he wanted the room's small tables and toys rearranged. And before anyone else could take action, the half dozen, jersey-wearing players, dwarfing the kids, began picking up or wheeling children, tables and chairs into place, as per Dak's specifications.

"We're going to strut our stuff, kids, in a hockey game. Unfortunately, the nurses wouldn't let us make an ice rink in here. And we had to leave our skates at the door. So-o-o..." He turned to the head nurse, who, with a grin, held out two jars, one containing tongue depressors and the other one cotton balls. "But the good news is we love hockey so much we can play it anywhere." He turned to the players, his dark eyes full of mischief. "Men, choose a stick."

Scratching his head as though he was confused, Dak asked the kids, "How many pucks should we have again?" He grabbed a handful of cotton balls. "This many?"

The children began laughing and yelling out numbers.

Landon stepped forward, raising his hand. "I'll be the goalie!"

"I'll be the other goalie," Mullens said, giving him a serious stare-down.

"You're not a real goalie. *I* am!"

"*Anyone* can play goal," Mullens said, bringing on the smack talk. He winked at Landon, silently telling him to go along with his banter.

"*Anyone* can play goal? You did not just say that." Landon expanded his shoulders, arms out as if he'd been offended and was ready to fight. "All *you* have to do is skate around and wait for the puck to come to you. I get *blasted* in the net!" He threw up his arms and turned to the kids, who joined his side, yelling at his teammate.

Mullens tried to hide a smile. "Fine, let's see if they call you The Blockade for nothin'." He tossed a tongue depressor at Landon. "You play *both* nets."

Landon widened his eyes at the kids, and Dusty held his gut, pointing and laughing. He hollered, "You can't play both! That's against the rules!"

"No, I'll play both. I can do this. I'll show these guys…." Landon fake glowered at Mullens. "You and your team are so going down."

His colleague laughed. "I'm gonna be on your side half the time."

"And my opponent the other half."

"I don't think this is gonna work, men," Dak announced loudly. He turned to the crowd. "What do you think? Could Landon be goalie for both teams?"

"Yeah!" the kids yelled.

Landon wasn't sure if they were just caught up in the excitement or if they truly didn't understand hockey. It was Texas, after all—the land of football and rodeo. Something the rookie, Leo, was already milking, showing off his shiny belt buckle to any kids—or nurses—who'd listen. The guy used to be a pro bull rider, and was always wearing a giant belt buckle, claiming it was a prize from some big rodeo or another.

Landon, having grown up in ranching country, knew the prestige some of those belt buckles carried, as well as the sacrifices Leo had made in order to win them. But it was way too much fun acting as though he was oblivious to how important they were to the guy.

Soon their makeshift hockey game was under

way, the men elbowing each other, and Landon slipping around in his socks as he hurried from net to net. The only good thing was that cotton balls were hard to slap shot and he could usually move faster than the fluffy puck.

Before long, the kids, realizing they could send players to the penalty box, had everyone but Landon sitting on the sidelines. Panting and sweaty, he begged one of the kids to call the game before letting any of his opponents out of the sin bin.

Dak saved him by announcing story time. Each player would take a child to his or her room and read a story, before heading back to the arena.

Mullens gave Landon a friendly clap on the back as he passed. "Good job."

He nodded, then sought out Dusty, who was looking wiped from all the excitement.

"Hey, kid. How's it going?" He scooped the boy into his arms, claiming him before another player did. There was no way he was reading to anyone else. Especially when they'd missed story time last night.

"Do you have to leave?" Dusty asked.

"Not yet."

"Good." The boy rested his head on Landon's shoulder, and a lump formed in the man's throat.

"Did you like our game?" he asked, as he padded down the long white hallway.

Dusty poked him. "You're silly."

"True." He stopped outside a door with a dinosaur painted above its number. "This your room?"

"Yeah." Dusty slid from Landon's arms and ran to his bed, where a Batman sticker book was lying open. Athena, during their dietician session yesterday, had dug through a box of books she said were for her new shop. She'd surfaced with this one for Dusty, having heard he was in the hospital and that Cass and Landon were juggling having someone there as much as possible during his waking hours, while also running the Christmas tree business. She'd assured him it would keep Dusty happy and busy.

It looked like the gift had been a hit, as there were Batman stickers everywhere. Stuck to the bed rails, food tray, guest chair, windows and walls.

"Look what Mom brought me! She said it's from you and Athena." He pulled a sticker off his bed's rail and slapped it onto the back of Landon's hand.

"Thanks, buddy. Yeah, Athena thought you might be bored. How are you feeling?"

Dusty shrugged. "I'm not really sick. Not like the other kids. They have cancer and stuff."

"Hopefully everyone will get better soon and be able to go home for Christmas." Another lump formed in Landon's throat as he thought about the holiday a little over two weeks away. "I hear we're supposed to read a story?"

"Yeah, you didn't read me one at bedtime last night."

"I was away at a game and you were here."

And that fact had sucked. He'd wanted to be here like a real dad would be. As if Dusty was his own kid.

It hurt just thinking about the kiddo being here without a dad.

They had just settled into a story when a loud alarm sounded.

Fire.

* * *

Cass was fixing the shelter she'd made out of an old tarp to block the direct afternoon sun from drying out her few remaining trees. They'd been selling well and the shallow trough she'd fashioned for the trees to stand in to absorb water was keeping them hydrated. Even though Prince Charming and the cats kept drinking out of it.

Cass glanced up from tying her last knot as a truck came flying down the driveway. She automatically scanned the yard for Rylnn, making sure she was off the road. The vehicle stopped, causing a cloud of driveway dust to carry past it. Jenny Oliver popped out, striding toward Cass in her tight Wranglers and bright Western blouse with pink stripes that matched her hairband.

"Did y'all hear?" she called. "I tried phoning, but it went to voice mail."

The concern in her friend's tone sent a wave of panic through Cass's nervous system. *Dusty? Landon?* "What's happened? What's wrong?"

"There's a fire at the children's hospital."

Cass gripped the corral railing for support. "What? When? Is everyone okay?"

Where was her phone? She needed her phone. Needed information, *now.*

"I just heard it on the radio in my store. I tried to call you, but when you didn't answer, I thought I'd better just drive out here."

"Thank you!" Cass swept her hands over her back pockets again, trying to locate her phone. She'd been so careful, keeping it on her while

Dusty was in the hospital. But she knew Landon was there this afternoon so she'd relaxed.

Landon... And Rylnn. She'd let the girl play a game on her phone over in the shade.

Why hadn't Landon called her?

Cass headed for the tree by the back porch. Rylnn was chasing Prince Charming around in circles, trying to coax the dog into pulling her wagon, probably so she could go to a pretend ball. The phone was sitting abandoned on the step.

She hurried toward it as Jenny's phone rang. "Hello? Yeah. I'm with her right now."

Cass spun toward her friend, who held out her phone. "It's for you."

She snatched the device, placing it to her ear, relaxing as soon as she heard Landon's voice.

"I don't know if you heard about the fire, but Dusty's okay. I'm here. Everyone's all right. The team evacuated his floor. We're in the parking lot waiting for the all clear."

She exhaled. "Thank you. Thank you, Landon."

"I tried calling you, but it went to voice mail."

Cass walked to her phone and flipped it over. Blank screen. Battery drained.

"I need to charge it. Are you sure everything's okay? Should I come in? I'm coming in."

"No, we're okay. I'm here and it sounds like we can go back in soon. There's no need to rush."

"How's Dusty? Is he freaking out?"

"The guys are all telling stories. He's having a blast, actually. And there's been no running, no exertion. We've been careful. Do you want to talk to him?"

"No, no. It's okay." She didn't want to draw more attention to the situation and make Dusty feel like it was a big deal and worth worrying over.

"Are you sure?"

She longed to hear her son's voice, to hear proof that he was indeed fine, but she trusted Landon. "Yeah."

"Because Maverick's telling tall tales about hitting flaming pucks into concession stands. You might actually save the kid from some mental warping."

Cass laughed. "No, it's fine. Thank you. And Landon?"

"Yeah?"

"Thank you for being there."

There was a pause before he said in a low voice, "No place I'd rather be."

And she believed it. Wholeheartedly. The man was as invested in Dusty as she was in Rylnn.

They were a family.

She let that sink in, then asked, "Hey, how did you know to phone Jenny?"

Her friend was listening, waiting as though she expected to be called into action.

"I was asking if anyone had some Sweetheart Creek numbers, and Dylan told me he had Jenny's. I figured it was worth a shot."

"Dylan O'Neill?" She glanced at Jenny.

The woman's cheeks turned pink and she rolled her eyes, shaking her head.

"Thank him, too, okay?"

She ended the call and faced her friend. "Why does the Dragons' center have your phone number?" she teased.

Jenny was looking to find love with Dylan? That? Yeah. Never happen. That would be a classic sunshine and grumpy bear scenario. Opposites attracting wouldn't come close to explaining the two of them.

"We met at Maverick's."

"Thanksgiving?" She'd heard the two had bickered the whole time. "And you were so taken with him that you gave him your phone number?"

Jenny rolled her eyes. "I told him to call me

sort of tongue in cheek. Daisy-Mae took me seriously and gave it to him."

"I thought Jackie was the town's matchmaker."

"She is. Oh, she is. Trust me. But Daisy-Mae's trying."

"And?"

"That man is exhausting."

"Exhausting? Hello! What does that mean?" Cass waggled her eyebrows.

"Always fighting." Jenny gritted her teeth and gently rammed her two fists together. But a tell-tale softening around her mouth hinted that maybe she hadn't minded the adversarial dynamic as much as she claimed.

"So? Have you two talked on the phone, then?"

Jenny turned bright red. "Once."

"And?"

"I doubt he'll ever call me again." Jenny's mouth twisted as she fought a smile.

Cass tried to hide her own amusement, but couldn't resist saying, "Okay, but just to let you know, I *am* creating a wedding venue here at Peppermint Lodge. There'll be some sweet discounts as I learn the ropes and get things going."

"Will not be needing them. Not with Dylan." Jenny glowered at her. "Although..." her tone turned sly "…you might be needing to book the space for yourself, hmm?"

Cass laughed. "No."

"Why not?"

She opened her mouth to explain how ridiculous it was to think that she and Landon had found love. It was pretend, but people didn't know that.

Sure, he was the kind of man she dreamed of. One who easily melded his way into her life, let her do her thing and was there when she needed him—like a freaking boulder, he was so reliable. Where it was just *easy*.

Cass closed her mouth. When had she fallen in love with Landon?

Wait. No. She wasn't in love. Not at all. What they had was purely platonic. That's what they'd agreed on, and that's the way it would stay.

And she was glad for it.

Wasn't she?

CHAPTER 12

"*P*lease come with me to the gala. Please?" Landon couldn't quite believe he was begging. If anyone had told him last summer that he'd be living with a beautiful woman and begging to take her to a ball, he'd have laughed and asked to have what they were having.

But here he was.

And he was quite definitely okay with it.

Then again, it could be the effects of the flu. The room still spun occasionally, and he felt slightly delirious.

But he was happy. Strangely happy.

Kind of like the kitten that had slipped in so

many times it had worn Cass down, and she'd finally allowed it to stay and snuggle with her.

Landon pulled the fuzzy blanket up to his chin, digging his shoulders deeper into the couch cushions beside Cass. The soft material felt so wonderful against his skin.

"Cass?" He glanced over. She was breathing like she was fighting nausea, even though neither of them had tossed their cookies in hours. They'd even got brave enough to brush their teeth, change their pajamas, have a snack, put on a new movie and ride out the end of their lingering fevers.

As soon as Cass had hinted that she felt under the weather, Alexa had whisked the kids over to her ranch, praying that Dusty wouldn't come down with anything. They needed him to stay strong and healthy until his surgery in two weeks.

Landon, in a moment of overconfidence borne of ample testosterone, and a faulty belief that he had an immune system made of steel, had offered to care for Cass, placing cool, wet cloths against her burning forehead.

Now they were sharing the cool cloth and playing paper-rock-scissors whenever one of them had to move off the couch for more ginger ale or to let the dog out.

Cass groaned, collapsing against his shoulder, strands of her curly hair plastered to her forehead. "I don't want to think or move or do anything. I'm achy."

"But dates are part of our new plus-one, fake-relationship agreement," he protested.

"I don't have a dress, and the gala is in five days." She stretched under the blanket, knocking it off his shoulders. He shivered and yanked it back, and she curled into his side, her long legs tucked against his.

"No dress, no problem."

"I'm not going naked!"

He laughed. "I'll buy you a dress, Cass." The Dragons' gala Christmas fundraiser was a black-tie affair. He'd be wearing a tux, but only if she was going to be on his arm.

"You can't keep throwing money at me." She pushed herself upright, her chest pressed into his shoulder as she stared at him. Having her in his personal space was only making him that much more certain that she needed to be his date.

"It's my prerogative. My tool. My contribution." He trailed a finger lazily up her leg and she shivered. "How about a gown with a slit up the side to show off your gorgeous long legs?"

She smiled and he did it again. She squirmed away, giggling. "Stop! My skin is super sensitive right now."

Ever since she'd made the fatal error of wandering into the kitchen in a shiny pink button-up pajama top and matching shorts, the slippery material revealing an expanse of leg, she was all he could think about.

She grabbed his hands, preventing him from moving in for another caress. He could break the hold, but liked having her fingers wrapped around his.

"Come with me." He leaned her way, nudging the side of her cheek with his nose. "Please, Cass."

She laughed and rolled away, but he tugged her back. "Let me pamper you."

"You want to take a cowgirl to a black-tie, fancy-pants thingy?"

"I like fancy pants. When I have you in a fancy dress, that is." She hadn't moved away, allowing him to nuzzle her cheek. He placed a light kiss at the edge of her mouth, testing his boundaries.

"What if I want to wear the fancy pants?" she asked, her tone breathless as she turned her head so they were forehead to forehead, their lips mere inches apart.

"Be my guest."

"Thank you."

"But so you know, there'll be hockey players present, so it won't be full-on, snooty affair. Just unruly, unmannered, stinky jocks playing dress-up."

She laughed, her warm skin pressing against him.

"I'm pretty sure at least one of us will show up with a cummerbund worn as a headband."

Cass smiled, curling against him, allowing her forehead to drift down to his cheek, and her jaw to rest on his shoulder.

"We could take bets," he suggested, wrapping an arm around her and pulling her against him. "Dibs on Mullens."

She giggled. "I'm sure that playboy has worn a tux a time or two."

"Doesn't mean the knucklehead knows how to wear one properly."

She was getting warm again and Landon folded the blanket down, grabbed the facecloth from the coffee table and held it to her forehead.

"That feels good."

"I hate going to stuff like that alone."

"Take Rylnn."

"Can't. As much as she'd love it."

Cass made a sound of acknowledgment.

"Jenny and Alexa have offered to babysit for us."

"You asked?" Her head popped up, and he dropped the cloth.

"Yes, because I know that once you hear that Daisy-Mae has a dress picked out for you, a babysitter will be your next excuse."

"I can't. Dusty's—"

"We won't be that far away. Alexa knows what to watch out for. Take a few hours for yourself before the surgery."

Her eyes met his, and he realized her lips were once again close enough to kiss.

"You really want me to come?"

He nodded.

"Why? Arm candy?"

He smiled.

She pressed a hand against his chest. "For real. Why?"

"Because I love you."

"You do?" Her eyes grew damp, her smile slightly soppy.

He held her close again. "I do."

"So do I."

"Is this just the fever talking for us?" he asked.

"Probably not."

They chuckled, as if sharing a joke, and cuddled closer, the TV droning on, ignored.

"I could wear Hannah's dress. Did you find my Halloween princess costume sexy?" There was a held-back giggle in Cass's voice.

Ah, yes. The puffy-sleeved affair that looked like it had been unearthed from the 1980s.

"You were very sexy. But the dress had nothing to do with it."

"*You're* sexy," she murmured sleepily, her hand roaming across his chest. "So many muscles." She ran her palm over the ridges of his abs, across the planes of his pecs, then down his side, sending tingles racing through him. "Do tuxes even fit over these muscles?"

He made a mental note to strut around the house shirtless and give her the full show. If he was going to be dreaming about her legs, it was only fair to be a good friend and return the favor.

"How do you give such amazing hugs with all this hardness?" She tapped his chest with a finger, smiling.

Her head was still tipped upward, and without thinking, he lowered his mouth to hers and kissed her softly. Her lips were warm, and she tasted tangy, like minty toothpaste and sweet ginger ale.

"I'm going to take *you* to that gala and you're going to be *my* arm candy," she said with a giggle. Her smile was slightly predatory and Landon hoped that this was the real Cass talking, not just her fever. Because he wanted nothing more than to continue right where they were currently leaving off.

* * *

Cass woke up with a lock of hair across her eyes. She sat up, brushing it away, before realizing she'd been curled against Landon on the couch.

He was pale, his long lashes dusting the shadows under his eyes.

Still sick.

She felt almost human again. Not too hot. Not too cold.

She lifted the facecloth off the blanket, setting it aside. It was dry now, no longer the cool relief Landon had plied to her skin over and over to bring her fever down.

She didn't know what she would have done without him.

He'd taken good care of her, to the point that

he'd gotten sick, too. He hadn't run away or barricaded himself—which he should have. He'd ended up missing work.

She wanted to curl back into his side, like a cat in a sunbeam, all happy and filled with gratitude for this man.

She'd needed him, and he'd been here.

Because they loved each other.

Landon's eyes opened and he smiled softly. "Hey."

"Hey."

"How are you feeling?"

"Better. You?"

Landon stretched his arms above his head, the fabric of his T-shirt pulling across his pecs.

She smiled lazily. His pecs. So firm. So…

Her smile dropped.

His pecs.

She remembered stroking his chest.

She'd been petting him. And those lips…

She knew what it felt like to kiss him.

She stood abruptly, her weak legs protesting the effort and sending her stumbling forward. She caught herself on the coffee table.

She'd kissed Landon. He'd told her he loved her.

She'd said it back.

No, not exactly like that, but the gist of it was they were in love with each other and had kissed, and that was all wrong. The only reason this thing between them worked was because they *weren't* in love.

Platonic.

It had to be platonic.

Stay there.

Be good.

She needed him.

She didn't need men.

Men left.

Oh, no. No, no. No.

"Where are you going? You okay?" Landon asked as she beelined from the room.

"Need a shower!" she called, before locking herself in the bathroom.

What had she done?

* * *

Alexa and Athena came out of Cass's room, grinning from ear to ear. Alexa was in jeans and an old sweatshirt, Athena in a gown that made Landon think of cocktails and smoky lounges from the seventies.

"Is she ready?" Landon put down the

Christmas snow globe he'd been mindlessly tumbling in his hands, and rose to his feet. He tried to avoid looking at his watch. He didn't care what time they got to the gala, but he'd been waiting for Cass to get ready long enough that his nerves had taken over.

He felt like a teenager waiting for his prom date.

Actually, no. He felt worse than that.

He remembered everything from having the flu with Cass. Everything. The caresses. The kisses. The professing of love.

And so did she.

He could tell by her skittishness, and the standoffish way she'd behaved ever since.

It was torture.

He wanted to carry on from flu day. He wanted to be able to kiss her, hold her hand, cuddle. Instead they were back to being the hockey player and the nanny. She was coming tonight because she'd made a promise.

Like a fool, he'd let loose and had spooked her.

"You'd better hang on to your jaw, because it's going to drop," Athena warned. She wrapped a fine, thin black scarf around her neck in the room's entry.

Cass's sister shrugged apologetically, flopping

onto the sofa beside the kids, who were playing a game on the iPad. "You can't take the farm girl out of her. Sorry, Landon. We tried."

"Oh, Lex!" Cass said with a heavy sigh, striding from her room. Her left leg appeared through the slit in her gown as she breezed past in stilettos, looking as if she'd been born to wear them and not her usual cowboy boots.

She was torturing him, right? The leg slit?

He watched her, on the lookout for an evil grin.

She wouldn't look at him.

Her glossy brown hair was swept high, a few wavy tendrils framing her face. Her eyes were done in a way that made her look like a mysterious supermodel, and her green gown, an off-the-shoulder number, shimmered under the living room's antler chandeliers and hugged her hips as she moved.

She was gorgeous.

And she'd never be his.

She snatched her checkered coat from its hook by the door, then turned and gazed at him expectantly.

He snapped into action. "You're ready? Okay, let's go."

"Be sure to stay out past her bedtime," Alexa cooed, giving them an innocent finger wave.

"No, not that!" Athena came hustling over before Cass could toss the grubby jacket over her dress. "Here." She slipped out of her own off-white coat, a mid-thigh wool number with a belt that cinched around the waist.

"But what will you wear to the gala?" Cass protested.

"I'll stop by the house and grab something else."

"But you planned your whole outfit. How are you going to snag your Professor Right?"

"Her what?" Landon asked.

"She wants a professor."

"Well, it's lucky most professors aren't fussy about looks," Athena said. "And there's no way you're wearing that old wreck over this gorgeous gown." She curled her lip as she shook out her coat and then held it up for Cass to slip into. She was a bit taller than Athena, the coat's arms a tad short if you looked carefully. But the impression she made was nothing short of stunning.

"Cassie!" Rylnn looked up, then tossed the iPad into Dusty's lap and zoomed off to her room. Seconds later she came flying back, clutching one of her princess tiaras. With a smile,

Cass crouched so the little girl could put it on her head.

Athena cringed, no doubt fearful of the impact Rylnn's tiara might have on Cass's perfectly done hair. She shook her head and opened the door. "I've got to run. See you two at the gala!"

"Thank you," Cass called as her friend headed out. She straightened, patting the tiara. "Perfect. Thank you, Rylnn."

"It's just borrowing," Rylnn said firmly.

"Yes, of course. I appreciate it."

Rylnn stood back, beaming at her. "We need pictures, Daddy!" She turned, grabbing at Landon's pocket, where he usually kept his phone. "Pictures, Daddy!"

Feeling self-conscious, Landon snapped one of Cass. It turned out blurry, and Rylnn gave him a dark look before snatching the phone and taking several more.

Cass slipped out of the coat and posed again.

"Smile, Cassie. Put your hand on your hip. Work it, girl."

Landon and Cass both laughed.

"Have you been watching that fashion model show again with Alexa?" Cass asked.

"Yup!" Alexa said. "It's our guilty pleasure, right Ry?"

"Cassie! Pose!"

Glowing, she complied, thrusting out a hip and making kissy faces that were surprisingly sexy.

Landon tried to sneak into one of the photos, but his daughter shoved him out of it. "Shoes." She snapped a photo of Cass's feet. "Rings."

"I'm not wearing any."

Landon found himself staring at her bare finger.

Patience.

He needed time to prove he wasn't leaving, and that she could count on him *and* his feelings.

"Okay, are we good?" he finally asked, stepping toward Rylnn, who turned toward him, snapping more photos. "That's enough."

"I'm favoriting them all, Daddy." She began tapping hearts for all the pictures, turning the hollow images red.

"We're going to be late."

"Now you, Daddy." She desperately waved Landon in beside Cass.

"Rylnn." She was loving the control of being their photographer, but they had to get a move on or they'd surpass being fashionably late.

"Daddy. You need pictures."

Shaking his head, and trying to ignore the way

Alexa was smirking, he gathered his patience and stood beside Cass.

Dusty came over, looking adorably sleepy. "Me, too!" He jumped into Landon's arms and Landon settled him on his hip. The boy smiled for two photos, then squirmed down and headed back to the iPad.

"Okay, that's good." Landon stepped toward the door, but Rylnn directed him back to Cass's side.

"Hold hands, Daddy."

His little wing-woman. He could hug her small misguided self.

"We're not holding hands," he said gently.

"Put your arm around her."

Cass finally looked at him. Carefully, he extended an arm, draping it across her shoulders. When she didn't balk, he leaned in, memories of them on the couch, cuddling, kissing, flooding his mind.

He subtly turned his head, inhaling her. She smelled nice. A hint of spruce tree and peppermint. Truly Cass through and through.

"Now kiss under the mistletoe," Alexa suggested in a teasing tone.

Landon dropped his arm.

"Where's your mistletoe, Cass? Somehow it

didn't get hung this year… Did it go missing in the move?" She shot her sister an innocent look, which Cass returned as a glare as she slid into Athena's borrowed coat.

"Phone." Landon put his hand out and Rylnn handed it to him. "And you?" He turned to Cass. "You should be in the car. We're late."

She saluted him seriously, then skipped out into the darkening night, seeming surprisingly happy to be dressed up and going out with him, even though she'd been avoiding him for days.

As Landon followed her to the door, Alexa called softly, "Don't be good."

If he could find a way to comply, he surely would.

***

"You look very nice," Cass said, brushing a hand across the shoulder of Landon's tux at the gala's coat check. She'd barely dared to glance at him since recovering from the flu.

She'd been too scared to.

When she'd left her room an hour and a half ago, fully primped by her sister and Athena, she'd peeked at him and instantly gone a bit wobbly. Afraid it would show, she'd acted eager to leave.

Get in the car so she could breathe again, sit. Recover from hotness overload. Spend incredible focus on extracting the tiara from her carefully done hair....

Because seriously, who put hot jocks in black tuxedos that had been *made* for them?

Who?

Killer tailors intent on slaughtering innocent farm gals such as herself who had never seen a living, breathing hunk like Landon waiting to take her to a formal affair. Like, seriously. Who?

The man should have a team of cardiologists trailing behind him with those shock paddles, reviving women in Landon's wake. Because wow.

And sitting in the car had not been a solution to the wobbly legs. Being so close that she could reach over and touch him? Torture. The scent of his soap, his...everything.

The worst.

And Rylnn? She'd been so sweet, but suggesting Landon hold her hand or put his arm around her? She was on Team Kill Cass, obviously.

The worst part was that Cass wouldn't have said no. She also wouldn't have turned away. That was the power of Landon in a tuxedo.

Not so fun when you were trying to remain standing, and strong. And…*platonic.*

Worst word in the English language.

But they couldn't act on their fever-induced feelings. It would ruin everything. She needed him and he needed her. The *kids* needed them.

There. Focus on the kids.

Not how cute their future ones would be should she and Landon get together.

"We look pretty hot, don't we?" Landon said.

"I might be coming down with something again," Cass said, cupping her forehead to gauge her temperature.

Felt normal.

But not on the inside.

Not at all.

She'd barely even noticed the gorgeous Christmas decorations in the ballroom and she *loved* everything Christmas.

Landon stepped closer, his feet bracketing her own. His hand was on her forehead before she could protest, the contact sending shivers through her. He gazed at her with concern, frowning. "You feel okay." He dropped his hand and held out his elbow. "Come on. I promised I'd be your arm candy. Once around the ballroom?"

She slipped her arm through his and took a steadying breath.

"We'll look back on Rylnn's photos when we're sixty," Landon said, "and claim that youth is wasted on the young."

"And complain how we never appreciated just how good-looking we were."

"Exactly." Landon smiled, the skin around his eyes crinkling as he gazed at her. The ballroom was packed, and they stopped just inside the doorway. "Maybe we should dance."

"Dance," she said, considering the idea. There was an ensemble playing something classical and people were waltzing. Or at least doing what she assumed was a waltz. Sort of an elegant two-step. And touching. Lots of holding each other. Dangerous, dangerous contact.

"We should claim a dance, since we aren't adequately appreciating our own hotness," Landon said.

"Right."

He was trying hard to loosen her up, shed the awkwardness that had developed between them over the past several days. If she wasn't careful she'd lose him by pushing him away. She needed to play light and easy, like she wasn't actually in love with him. Just carry on. Be friends. Keep doing this co-parenting thing they were so good at.

"We'll be able to say we drank in life through a wide straw, and that we enjoyed every drop of our evening," she said decidedly.

"Tall order." He took her hand with a smile, the relief that she was playing along with his game almost palpable. "We'd better get cracking."

"Drink all the free champagne."

"Bid on everything in the silent auction."

"What if we win it all?"

"Then that's a life fully lived, wouldn't you say?" His hand went to her waist, and she focused on their banter rather than how good it felt to have him touch her, to feel him so close, to draw in his strength, his presence.

She was his *date.*

"We'll laugh at everyone's jokes and smile until our cheeks hurt," Landon murmured, leading her onto the floor.

"Dance until our feet ache."

"Shut down the party."

"Make friends with the band." She glanced at the white-haired musicians hunched around their instruments behind their music stands.

"Living it up?" Landon asked with a smile. Her

hand fit so perfectly into his, her hand so natural on his shoulder.

"I don't know. If I recall you need a lot of breaks when you're out on the dance floor."

He laughed good-naturedly at her reference to Rylnn dancing him off his feet last May.

"Hey, how is your ankle, anyway?" Cass peered down at the same time he did, bumping heads with him. "Ow."

"You okay?" Landon's hand left her waist and he rubbed his forehead. Then he brushed a lock of hair away from her own.

"Fine. You?"

"Yeah. You sure?"

She nodded, and they continued to dance in silence.

She'd needed this tonight. Needed Landon and the uplifting breath of fresh air and ease he brought with him. No thinking about Dusty or his upcoming surgery. No freaking out over fever-induced I-love-you's. Just she and Landon hanging out like old times, because everything was better with him.

"Cutting in." Mullens, without another word, wedged himself between Landon and Cass.

"Did I say yes?" she asked. "I'm not a *thing*, you know."

The big hockey player grinned and spun her away from a stunned and slightly miffed looking Landon.

"I was dancing with my date."

"Trust me on this," Mullens said, smiling down. He was a very tall man. He leaned in like he was going to whisper something in her ear, but didn't. It left her feeling slightly unstable and very aware of him.

Cass glanced in Landon's direction. His hands were in fists and his cheeks and neck red.

Oh.

"Put your hand on the back of my neck and we'll dance a little closer," Mullens suggested.

She kept her hand on his shoulder. "What are you up to? Didn't I see Athena throw her drink on you earlier?"

"No."

He provided no further answer, just danced them closer to where Landon was waiting at the edge of the floor. Mullens's body was so close she could feel the heat of him. She knew the game he was playing and immediately felt bad for Landon.

"It's not him. It's me," she said quietly.

"I know."

"But you're taunting him."

"Yes."

"Why?"

Mullens met her eyes. "Sometimes a woman needs help to see the strength of the truth she's denying."

"What truth? That he wants something we can't have?"

"And why can't you have it?" he asked mildly.

"One of us has to be practical."

He dropped his head back and laughed. "Cass, hon, what does practicality ever have to do with love?"

She felt her cheeks heat. "We have kids."

"And what's better for them to witness?"

"What?"

"Is it better seeing you claim love? Or denying it for their 'benefit'?"

"Mullens, it's not like that!"

But it was, wasn't it? She wasn't modeling what she wanted for the kids when they became adults. In fact, it wasn't about them at all. It was about her and her own stupid fears.

The kiss and I-love-you's weren't fever-induced. They'd been real. Genuine.

She loved Landon.

They were practically dancing in front of him now, and Mullens called, "Ankle's still bugging you, huh? Too bad."

He spun Cass again, as though showing off, then launched her straight into Landon's waiting arms. He caught her expertly, his hands braced along her back like he was going to dip her, his lips almost on hers. Then, his eyes locked on hers, he elegantly dipped her backward in a smooth move that felt sensual.

Cass wished he'd be brave for both of them, ignore her signals and just kiss her.

* * *

Landon danced Cass away from Mullens as swiftly as he could without either of them stumbling. He knew the guy was messing with him, and that his teammate knew just how under his skin he'd gotten.

That wasn't the worst part, though. The worst was that Cass had put on the brakes after they'd had the flu, and he didn't know how to persuade her to release them.

But at least now she was back in his arms, smiling shyly, cheeks flushed.

And dang it, why *were* her cheeks so pink, as if she'd enjoyed being flirted all over by that big, worthless goon?

"What?" he asked, the word sounding like he'd

bitten it off. "You enjoyed dancing with that retro playboy?"

"Retro?" She glanced in Mullens's direction and laughed. "What *is* that man wearing?"

His seventies-style tuxedo was a statement, if nothing else.

"Show-off," Landon muttered.

"He and Athena both have that flair," Cass mused. "They can put on clothes from any decade and make it work. It's magic."

"It's voodoo. The way he goes through women is disgusting."

Cass's eyebrows shot up. "You know I came here with you, right?"

Landon's shoulders sank down a notch, and the fuel feeding his inner fire eased up slightly.

"He seems fun," she stated, "but he's not my type... Unless, of course, he needs a nanny."

Landon's grip on her waist had tightened involuntarily, but Cass laughed. "You know I go home with you," she added.

It took Landon a moment to register the underlying tone in her words, and he snapped his attention to her face. Her eyes were shining and filled with...hope?

I go home with you.

If he didn't know better, he'd think she wanted him to kiss her.

Her hand, which had been on his shoulder, slid to the back of his neck, making him shiver. He pressed his cheek to her hair and slowed their steps. Dancing was good, an excuse to get close without complicating things.

But the way she'd just been looking at him—that would definitely complicate things. What had Mullens done to her? In a minute flat she'd gone from skittish to…whatever this was.

What was real? What should he act on? The stakes were dangerously high if he got this wrong.

"Makes you wonder why he's like that," Cass said. "Why he teases."

"Not really."

"You're not curious?" She lifted her head to look at him. "I sometimes wonder what shaped you into such a kind and caring man. Like, what made you able to predict my problems, and be ready to solve them before they bring me down. You tease out the best in me. You make me stronger."

Landon gave her a curious glance. This felt very close to an I-love-you.

She snuggled in again. "I feel like I have a chance to be a better mom because of you."

"What do you mean? You're a great mom."

"I don't know." She seemed to struggle with finding the right words. "It just feels like a second chance."

He'd been aware of how worry had worn at her resiliency as they drew closer to Dusty's very expensive and invasive surgery—only a week and a half away. And how fighting the flu had knocked back her reserves.

She wasn't looking for love and she wasn't looking for a kiss. She was admitting she was ready to lean on someone strong instead of facing the storm alone.

If she was also sending subtle, flirtatious invitations it was only because she was looking to forget. To live in the moment and leave behind the pain and uncertainty that had enveloped her life.

No hanky-panky. That was one of her firmest ground rules.

She *was* vulnerable right now. Scared, and looking to him for that warm, secure feeling. He would not take advantage of that. He would be the man she needed. Unshakable. Here. Present.

Now, tomorrow and until Dusty was back on his feet. And if she'd let him, even longer than that.

Landon pulled her against him, holding her, rocking her as they slow danced, longing to tip her chin upward and press a gentle kiss on her lips.

But the one thing he would not do was make a move on her when she was in a less-than-rock-solid emotional state—even if it meant keeping himself very busy or even going back home for Christmas, so he'd be removed from temptation.

CHAPTER 13

"*N*o. Go." Cass avoided looking at Landon, and closed the oven door a little too hard, rattling the burners as she checked on the casserole. She dropped her holly-print oven mitts on the counter and turned up the Christmas song playing on the kitchen radio.

"You sure you'll be okay?"

"Of course. We got along fine before you moved here."

A few nights ago, at the gala, she'd sent him signals to kiss her. Kiss her!

And ever since then she'd gotten the vibe that he thought she was fragile and couldn't take care of herself and Dusty.

But now, instead of being Mr. Fix-It-and-Be-

Present, like she expected, he was planning to skedaddle out of here for the holidays. Retreat all the way to Canada to avoid spending his three days off with her.

Honestly, she'd known it was coming. She'd just managed to convince herself that Landon was different, because she'd been lonely and a bit scared. She'd wanted him and their feelings to be genuine and true.

Yet here they were, as predictable as an interstate across the plains of the Midwest. Get close, but when challenges looked like they were closing in, pull back. And things were about to get seriously rough in a week, when her son had his surgery.

Landon had acted so great with Dusty because it was who he was. He gave to everyone in his life, but that didn't mean he wanted to be Dusty's new daddy.

He was Rylnn's dad because his best friend, Zofia, had asked him to be the sperm donor. He'd never intended to be a real father, but had stepped up to the plate when she passed on because he was Landon. It's what he did: rocked whatever challenge was thrown at him.

That didn't mean Cass should put another kid

in need on his shoulders, just because he was a nice guy.

He'd pulled back when she'd given him signals, and there was a reason for that. A reason she might not understand but needed to respect.

"Dusty's surgery is coming up fast," Landon said carefully. "Ry and I don't have to go."

"Go see your family. You don't need permission from me."

So what if she'd assumed Landon and Rylnn would be here for Christmas, and that they'd all go to the community Christmas concert? It wasn't like she'd planned baking, movies, games and activities to fill the three days off, as they celebrated the holiday together like one big happy family.

She marched out of the kitchen, frustrated at the way she'd gotten her hopes up. Landon followed.

Cass stopped in front of the Christmas tree, not wanting to face him or show the depth of her hurt and disappointment.

As promised, she'd taken the crushed spruce and set it up in the living room. She'd turned the battered side to the corner, but the tree somehow looked worse than ever today, leaning crazily as if the kitten had been climbing it again.

It didn't help that when she looked at it Cass could still feel the phantom weight of Landon landing on top of her. How could she still experience the gravity of that moment, the way their eyes had connected, as though truly seeing each other as more than a parent, more than someone helping hold the seams of their lives together?

How could that not have been real?

And Prince Charming. Dammit, but she missed that giant dog. Brant had found him a home and had picked him up two days ago, only adding to her angry, frustrated mood. The kids had cried for hours, and there had been nothing she could do, since she couldn't afford the Great Dane's enormous food bill. And she wasn't about to ask Landon to pay for it. Because once he left —which he seemed to be gearing up to do—she'd be screwed.

She yanked on the scraggly Christmas tree, trying to straighten it. It was nothing like the gorgeous trees at the gala. The ballroom had been beautifully decorated, and she wanted her own lodge to be like that one day. Warm and cozy, with a million decorations, filled with wonderful scents of peppermint and live Christmas trees, love, laughter and family.

She adjusted a few decorations the kids had

made, trying to ignore the fact that Landon was standing behind her, drilling her with what she knew would be questioning looks.

She'd believed he was going to kiss her at the gala on Friday, but then he'd pulled back and started treating her as though she was fragile.

Saturday, on his way out the door to an away game, he'd mentioned spending Christmas in Canada. Then he'd had another game on Sunday night.

Now it was Monday, and while there was no game today, he was leaving for practice in a minute. He'd have one other away game, then suddenly it would be Christmas, and he and Rylnn would be gone.

Then back for another game, followed by a day off, and suddenly it would be the twenty-ninth, the day of Dusty's surgery.

"I'll ask for time off next week," Landon offered, his voice low and gravelly.

"You can't miss more games." She turned from the tree, hands on her hips.

"I've missed only one."

"Three. You got the flu, remember?" He'd taken care of her and gotten sick, instead of wisely skedaddling like the kids had. At the time she'd been delighted that he cared and was there for her. But now… Now she saw that he didn't think she could take care of herself and that she was fragile. And maybe she was. She was terrified about Dusty, but that didn't mean Landon had to suddenly start treating her differently. "You can't ignore your career."

"I'm not."

She pulled the gray-and-white kitten from within the Christmas tree's branches, sending an ornament tumbling to the floor, where it broke. Cass cursed silently, straining for patience.

"Don't take time off for us," she grumbled, pushing the kitten into Landon's arms on her way past him to retrieve a broom.

"Cass. This is important."

She turned to face him, her anger rising. "He's my kid, Landon. You're not his dad. You're off the hook. I've got this. So just go! Go to Canada and do your job."

Landon flinched as if he'd been struck. He put the kitten down on the couch with extra care. "Fine." He lifted his hands in surrender and backed away. "I won't take time off for Dusty's surgery."

He snatched his workout bag and strode from the room, not even saying goodbye to the kids before he climbed into his SUV and drove off.

Cass, steadying her nerves, wished she could reverse the past few days and put their lives back on the rails again.

* * *

"What's your problem?" Maverick asked, skating past Landon, who was standing at the net. He slid to a stop, sending a spray of ice shavings flying. "You aren't blocking a thing. And you went after Mullens for no reason."

"Sorry, Cap."

"Don't give me that captain crap. I'm serious. What's the deal?"

Landon clenched his jaw and got low in the net, ready for the next slap shot. Practice wasn't that long, but today's felt like it had gone on for eight or nine hours.

Cass was pushing him away.

He's my kid.

It was like Landon didn't even count anymore. Like she didn't see that he was worried sick about the boy's surgery and wanted to be there. Not just for her and Dusty, but because he cared. Deeply.

She thought he was ignoring his career for them. No, he was being a family man. He was putting them first. Didn't she see that?

Wasn't that what women wanted?

A puck ricocheted off his helmet, making his ears ring.

Landon crouched lower, ready for the next shot, his quads burning.

Was she so independent, and so certain that every man was like her ex, that she couldn't see him? He was right in front of her, and he was different.

He hadn't really planned to go home at Christmas. He'd been bluffing.

And she'd practically booked his ticket back to Canada for him.

Sure, he'd love to see everyone again, even though it had been only two months since he had. But having only three days off meant he and Rylnn would be spending more time in airports and sleeping than they would with family.

Family.

He caught the next puck and dropped it behind the net, then got back into position.

Cass and Dusty were family.

He *knew* she was vulnerable and freaked out right now, so he needed to be patient.

He blocked a shot with his wide shin pad. The next slipped through the gap between his left leg and outstretched arm.

Dusty's surgery was in a week.

One. Week.

He missed saving the next five shots, and Louis sent him to skate laps.

Which only served to give him more time to stew.

* * *

Cass paced the waiting room, ignoring the handsome, brooding man sitting in the corner jiggling his leg. She hated that, despite it being only four days post-Christmas, the area was still decorated for the holidays. She didn't want her anxiety and fear to be wrapped up in her favorite time of year, tainting it forever.

Not that it had been much of a holiday. She'd gone through the motions, her thoughts and worries overriding the joy of time spent with her son, her sister and brother-in-law.

Landon popped up from his chair and paced to the vending machine. When he gripped its sides and bowed his head, his suit jacket pulled at his shoulders and his white dress shirt became untucked, revealing a flash of skin at his side. He straightened, then turned to face her. "How much longer?"

"You need to catch your plane," Cass stated. As a compromise, she'd told him he could come wait during the surgery, but he couldn't miss his game. And his flight to the away game left in an hour.

"I need to be *here*."

"It shouldn't be much longer," Alexa said, checking her watch.

Landon sank back in the chair, and Cass sat beside him. "You can go. We're okay."

"I need to know how he is."

She took him in, from his pale face to the sweat along his brow. He looked like he hadn't slept at all. The six of them—Cass, Landon, Dusty, Rylnn, Cash and Alexa—had stayed at Landon's condo last night, where Cash was currently hanging out with Rylnn.

"I can call you," Cass said gently. "Go."

Landon rubbed a hand down his face. "No." He shook his head, pushing further into the chair as if he expected someone to pull him out against his will. "I won't be any good to the team unless I'm here. Unless I know."

Cass studied him, realizing how true that was. The man was a wreck. She should be freaking out herself, but somehow she was simply numb, the entire morning feeling like she'd been moving in a weird bubble, not quite connected to reality.

Landon's leg started jiggling again.

This man loved her son. Not for any reason or obligation other than he simply did.

She slipped her hand into his and squeezed. He gripped back with both hands.

She'd hardly seen Landon since the gala, given his insane schedule. They'd barely talked, and she realized how much she'd missed him. She was about to tell him as much when she heard her name being called.

"Ms. McTavish?" the doctor repeated, scanning the room. She spotted Cass and began moving toward her.

Cass stood, her legs suddenly shaky with adrenaline and fear. She opened her mouth to speak, but her throat locked. Landon rested his hand on her shoulder, a reassuring, calming weight.

The surgeon smiled. "He's asking for his mom."

Cass's eyes grew wet and she held back a sob. Her baby was alive. Awake. Asking for her!

The bubble she'd been in broke and she shuddered, her legs giving out, every emotion from the past several weeks shoving their way through her, leaving her head and heart reeling.

Landon's arm went around her, and his

soothing voice scattered everything but joy and gratitude as he asked, "How did it go? Can we see him?"

"It went really, really well. We expect a full recovery and a normal life without restrictions." Her tone turned cautionary. "Of course, he's not out of the woods yet. We'll keep him here a few days to make sure he doesn't develop an infection and that everything continues to look good."

"Can we see him?" he repeated.

The woman nodded. "He's also asking for Landon?"

"That's me," he said quickly.

"I'm sorry." She checked her clipboard. "Family only."

Cass gripped his hand. "He is family."

"Immediate family," the doctor said apologetically.

Cass felt Landon's grasp slip in hers.

"He's his stepdad," she lied, giving his fingers a squeeze.

"In that case, follow me."

* * *

Stepdad.

The word repeated over and over in Landon's

head as they followed the surgeon to the recovery room, where Dusty was waiting for them.

Cass had lied to the doctor.

Lied for him.

No, for Dusty.

The boy came first. This wasn't about her wanting to give him that title.

Even though he'd be a fantastic stepdad.

Maybe she knew that, and was just scared. He could see it in her eyes sometimes. The fear. The pulling back. The catching herself. The reminders that all of what they had was too good to be true.

But it wasn't.

It was good *and* it was true.

And it was theirs. He just had to find a way to calm her fears and make it so.

He squeezed her hand.

He couldn't tell her that he loved her, that he wanted to be part of her family. Not right now. She'd think it was just the stress talking.

He'd let Dusty recover and life return to normal. Then Landon would show her how he really felt.

He'd convince her that he'd been created solely for the purpose of loving her, and that only he could love her the way she was meant to be loved.

The doctor paused in a doorway, gesturing for Cass and Landon to enter.

Cass rushed to the bedside, and Landon took a moment to deal with the lump in his throat at seeing the boy looking so small and fragile.

Dusty's eyelids were droopy and machines surrounded him. Tubes wound their way out from underneath the sheet, and an oxygen mask covered most of his face, but he broke into a smile when he saw them.

Landon found himself grinning back and came to stand behind Cass, giving her shoulder a caress.

The short visit passed in a blur, and soon Cass was tugging on Landon's elbow, telling him he had to get to his game. They kissed the sleepy boy and moved out into the hallway.

Landon felt like he was walking on air. The weight of the morning had lifted, and he turned, moving backward down the hospital corridor and snatching up Cass's hands in his. "He's going to be okay. Our boy is going to be okay." Grinning, he grabbed her and swung her around in the middle of the hallway.

Her laugh was muffled against his chest until, with reluctance, he slowly set her back on her feet.

"Go win him a game tonight," she said, smoothing his suit jacket.

Everything was going to be okay.

Feeling resolve, he gently tapped her on the nose and said, "Your wish is my command, Princess Cowgirl."

CHAPTER 14

Cass dropped her purse on a battered table near the back of Sweetheart Creek's town office meeting room. It wouldn't be long until the place was stuffed with citizens ready to debate tweaks and changes people wanted to make to their properties or businesses.

She needed to get a business permit, as well as have the Peppermint Lodge rezoned so she could start holding weddings there. It had once been zoned commercial, but had been switched back before she'd moved in. Tonight she'd make her pitch, settle any apprehension from neighbors, hand in her paperwork and keep her fingers crossed that the council voted yes on her proposals.

What would she do if they said no?

She had a half-renovated lodge. Well, half-gutted and in need of flooring, paint, furniture and so many other things before summer. She was feeling the heat, not just because the cost of Dusty's surgery and care had been astronomically high—leaving her insurance payouts and the Dragons' charity's donation in the dust when it came to coverage—but also because Maverick and Daisy-Mae had gotten engaged on New Year's Eve and told the press they were having their wedding at her lodge.

Her lodge.

Her destroyed, ratty building that needed years of TLC was going to host a celebrity wedding.

People had been coming out of the woodwork, calling her, begging to help work the wedding. She should say yes even though a date hadn't yet been set. Maybe they'd show up early and work for free.

Her to-do list was eight hundred miles long and the entire world around her had gone insane.

It was like life had been on pause while Dusty was waiting for surgery, and now that he was home and mending quickly, the Universe had lifted its finger off the button and accidentally hit Fast Forward instead.

Which was good. It gave her less time to think about Landon. And those simmering looks filled with meaning. Or the longing.

Or thinking about what it might be like if he said yes to that shaving commercial and appeared shirtless on TV as well as online, turning himself into a sex symbol overnight. Cass wasn't sure she could handle that. Women drooling, throwing themselves at him even more.

What if he chose one of them? What if he brought her home?

But those looks he'd been shooting Cass lately… He'd gone from practically avoiding her to heated glances brimming with meaning.

Was it because Dusty was medically out of the woods and she no longer needed to lean on Landon emotionally that he was all systems go?

She didn't think so.

But why didn't he just say he loved her, give her a giant kiss and be done with all this uncertainty?

"Hey," Athena said, dropping into the chair beside her. "Wow. You look exhausted. How's Dusty?"

"Really well. I didn't realize how slowed down

he was due to his health problems. It had been so gradual, you know? And now he's so full of beans." She smiled, thinking of how he'd *wanted* to go for a bike ride with Rylnn and Landon to the end of the driveway last night.

She'd been nervous. Was it too much, too soon?

But Landon had checked the sheet from the surgeon and assured her that it would be okay. He'd be there to ensure Dusty didn't ride too hard or too fast with his newly increasing energy.

Her boy was so happy. So filled with life.

It made her smile. Every day.

He was going to be all right.

"Then?" Athena prompted.

"I know why she's exhausted," Hannah said, sliding into the seat on Cass's opposite side. She waggled her eyebrows.

Cass scowled, and Hannah's shoulders dropped. "Really? You haven't told him yet?"

"Told who what?" Athena asked, leaning forward.

"Athena, why are you here?" Hannah asked. "I'm here because Edith asked me to do her job and submit a permit to expand the daycare." She pulled a face.

"What's going on?" Athena asked, tugging at

Cass's sleeve. "Why did she change the subject? Is this about Landon? Are you breaking up?"

"What *are* you here for, Athena?" Hannah asked her cousin.

She held up paperwork. "Grand opening for The Huckleberry Bookshop." She turned back to Cass. "What haven't you told the mysterious '*him*'?"

"You don't need permission for a grand opening," Hannah argued.

"Liquor license. And we also need to pour into the street for a few activities." She shrugged. "Need approval for an 'event,' according to Henry."

Hannah scrunched up her nose. "Ignore him. He's even worse now than when we were kids."

"Tell me about Landon."

"Shh. The meeting's starting." Hannah folded her hands on the tabletop and turned to the front of the room, while Athena shot both of them another puzzled look.

Before long, Cass was up at a microphone talking about her plans for her event center, the upcoming wedding and rezoning. The old man with flyaway hair began grumbling louder than he had during Hannah's proposed daycare expansion.

"Plans to destroy the town," Henry muttered. "All those hockey players."

Cass wrapped her hands tight around the base of the microphone, imagining it was his neck. "Excuse me, sir, did you have something to add?"

He turned to her, eyes narrowed. "A wedding center? What do you know about weddings? This town can't handle something big like that. We don't even have enough hotels."

Cass swallowed. It was true. All of it, possibly.

The town's new mayor sighed and tiredly waved him to the second microphone. "Henry, stand up to the mic, please. No heckling. There's a process here."

"Some guests will stay at the lodge," Cass said, her heart beating hard, as if the man had told her she'd never find love again. That she wasn't worthy.

Somehow her own feelings about love had gotten twisted up in opening the lodge to brides and grooms. She needed to separate, focus.

"It'll be like a bed-and-breakfast."

"So you plan to take business away from the town's motel, do you?" Henry asked, speaking into the other microphone.

Cass bit her tongue about the motel at the end of Main Street. Its sign still boasted that it now had air-conditioning and Wi-Fi. The place was dated and lacked a certain curb appeal. She was pretty sure people would rather sleep in a tent on the lodge's lawn than stay there.

That was an idea. She could bring in old caravans for people to sleep in, and convert the backs of old pickup trucks into tent platforms for the more adventurous.

"You're going to ruin this town," the man grumbled.

"I don't believe we've met," she said clearly. If he wanted to battle, she was more than ready. She had almost a month's worth of sexual frustration she could channel into arguing.

Using her height to her advantage, she straightened her spine as she crossed the row of seats separating the two microphones to stand before him, hand extended. "Cassandra McTavish."

He gave it a quick shake. "Henry Wylder."

She smiled sweetly. "Pleasure to meet you, Henry."

"Good luck getting the permits you need to run this town into the ground."

"Henry, give it a rest," Athena said, her tone hinting at restrained exasperation.

"You and your porn shop," Henry muttered at her.

"It's a bookstore and café!"

"We won't approve the permit to open it."

"It's already been passed," one council member said tiredly. "Unanimous. No, sorry. There was one nay."

"As always," someone else muttered, scowling at Henry.

"Don't take him personally," Hannah said as Cass sat down again, her permit and rezoning application submitted for final approval. "His bark is way worse than his bite."

"Too bad the same can't be said for me," Cass whispered with a laugh, determined to make a go of the lodge now more than ever.

As the meeting continued on, Athena huddled closer, dropping her voice. "Okay, tell me about the problems you're having with Landon. Because you two are meant to be."

"I know that. But I don't think he does," Cass whispered back.

"*I* think he does," Hannah said, blessedly not filling Athena in on what Cass had divulged at the hockey game on New Year's Eve.

Dusty had still been in the hospital, and Hannah had convinced her to take a short break away from sitting with him to bring Rylnn to the game. The girl had been having a tough go being shuffled between people all week. In a moment of weakness, Cass had confessed to her friend that her relationship with Landon was fake, and that she was in love with him.

Looked like she planned to never let that go.

"Yeah, we connect, Landon and I. But he doesn't love me, Hannah. Not like that," she said.

"Have you seen the way he looks at you?" Athena squeaked, with a laugh loud enough to draw the attention of more than a few council members. "Sorry," she muttered, sinking lower in her chair.

"How can you say that?" Hannah hissed. "His love is in everything he's done for you and Dusty."

"Why is he still sending me all these mixed signals? It's like every week is different." Cass rubbed her forehead. "I'm so confused. He told me he loved me, but he was feverish at the time. I thought we were going to, I don't know…date? And then we just sort of… It all fell apart." She sighed.

"Love is complicated," Athena said, raising her hand. She elbowed Cass with her other arm. "Vote!"

Cass's hand shot up, even though she had no idea what the issue was. "At the gala I thought we were going to finally commit," she admitted when the voting was done. "You know. For real."

"For real?" Athena's eyes narrowed.

"But then he started treating me like I was fragile."

"You were," Hannah stated. "That was right before the surgery. You were totally fragile."

"Maybe he was afraid you were falling into him for the wrong reasons," Athena suggested. "You know. He seemed good enough because you needed help and he was there?"

"Okay, sure. I could see that. But still. Why would he stay for a kid that's not his? Why would he stay when Dusty's real dad wouldn't?" It felt so wholly unfair and confusing. "Why is he putting so much into us when it's so incredibly hard every day?"

"Maybe it's not that hard."

"It is." There was no doubt about it. But life was way easier with Landon there. "What if he leaves us?"

Her friends were silent.

"Why hasn't he already? It got tough and he went away. What if he does it again?"

"Cass," Hannah stated, her tone stern, "he visited family at Christmas. You can't hold that against him. Especially when he was there, with you, for the surgery."

She nodded. "You're right. You're right. I'm losing my mind."

"Think about it, Cass. What could be harder than being there at the hospital?"

Nothing. Nothing could be harder than that.

The knowledge hit her hard: Landon wasn't going anywhere. Not for anything.

And maybe he truly had been afraid that she was choosing him for the wrong reasons. For convenience and not for love.

"Why is he still here?" she asked softly, mulling over the idea that he might truly love her and Dusty. "Still helping?"

What made one man stay when another couldn't or wouldn't?

"Because, Cass," Athena said firmly, "some men know how to love."

* * *

"Landon?"

"In here," he called to Cass. He lifted his headphones off his ears, pausing the sound bath Coach Louis had given him and the other players.

It was calming, and it slowed the voices and doubts in his head. Some days it even quelled his impatience to tell Cass that he loved her for real, and to hurry up and get over herself and let herself love him back.

They were meant to be.

He knew it.

She knew it.

Everyone knew it.

How many steamy looks did a man have to give a woman before she released her barriers and opened up and said yes?

"I paid the hospital," he said, as soon as she appeared in his doorway, figuring that was the reason for her take-charge tone. He sat on the edge of his bed, bare toes toying with the area rug's soft fringe.

"What?" Her face blanked.

Okay, so apparently she hadn't received the hospital's paid-in-full receipt yet.

"What's up?" he asked, suddenly curious about her determined look and what had actually spurred it.

"Wait. You paid for the surgery?" She kept her voice low, as though the kids playing in the living room would overhear—or care.

"I got an advance on that commercial deal."

"What? I thought you didn't want to be exploited."

"I took it for Dusty." *For you.*

"But… You had this whole speech about being a role model and not taking your shirt off to sell products."

He chuckled at her serious tone. "Yeah, putting the daddy in dad bod." He winked at her and her cheeks went pink, her eyes drifting to his chest. There was a glint of fire in them and, if he wasn't mistaken, a hint of possessiveness as well.

"That's going to be so weird for Rylnn," she whispered.

"Yeah, but she wasn't who I was thinking about with the role model stuff."

Cass shook her head as though trying to shuttle her thoughts into order.

"I didn't want to add to our society's toxic masculinity," he explained, "and the idea that you're not a real man if you're not muscle-bound, without an ounce of fat."

Her pale brown eyes went soft.

He stood, feeling suddenly self-conscious. "So we found a work-around."

"What does that mean?"

"I'll keep my shirt on."

He could have sworn she let out a breath of relief.

The shaving company hadn't been happy, but they'd agreed when he'd said he'd take 20 percent less for the deal.

"You overwhelm me." Cass exhaled, pushing a hand through her hair.

"You two need a fresh start." No debt. A beautiful lodge. Good health.

Her attention cut to him, her jaw dropping in what might have been shock and hurt. "Don't leave." Her words were quick, the look in her eyes one of fear.

"Cass…"

Her eyes filled with tears. "Please. I'm sorry."

"For what?"

"For not…" She blinked, glanced up at the ceiling and sniffed.

"Why do you think I'm leaving?"

"I saw the rental listings on the coffee table earlier."

"It's for Mullens."

"What?"

"He was asking about the town. It's the stuff from when I was looking back in October."

"Oh." She blinked again. "But that's out-of-date."

He shrugged. "Mullens always lands on his feet. If there's a penthouse in town, he'll find it."

Landon gave Cass a soft smile, moving closer. "Do you want me to stay?" He rubbed a hand down her arm.

She nodded.

She didn't say anything further, so he stepped back, not wanting to pressure her. "Then we'll stay."

Her fingers tangled in the fabric of his soft sweater and she yanked him forward. And then his lips were on hers in a glorious kiss.

He broke it, meeting her eyes, trying to read more. "You sure about this, cowgirl?"

"I've wanted to do this since the gala," she confessed, pulling him close again.

"I know," he said, before stealing another kiss.

She gave him a light shove, just hard enough to show her frustration with him. "Then why have you been acting all squirrelly?"

"I haven't been. It just hasn't seemed like a good time. I was afraid that..." He sighed, not quite wanting to say the words out loud.

"You thought I only wanted a warm body?"

"Maybe?" He winced at her wounded expression. "Hey, be fair! You're not great at the whole emotions thing, or needing other people, or letting them in, or trusting that they'll stick around when the going gets tough." Realizing he was holding his forearms between them like a shield, he relaxed, putting his arms where he really wanted them—around Cass.

She nodded, her jaw set. "You're right. I suck at this."

"No, no. You were going through a lot. You mean too much to me to chance it. To screw it up."

Her shoulders relaxed.

"Do you trust me?" he asked.

"Yes!"

"Like me?"

"The only warm body I'll ever want is yours," she said, snuggling against him.

He tipped her chin up and pressed his lips gently to hers. She took over the kiss, quickly turning it from gentle and sweet to hungry and intense.

They stumbled, finding a wall to prop themselves against as his fingertips skimmed up her body, tracing her curves. Her hands were under his shirt, dancing over his muscles, possessive, wanting.

"I love you," she said, her lips moving down his jaw. Then, as though catching up with her words and thoughts, she tipped her head back to look at him. "I wasn't just saying that when we were sick on the couch, either."

"Good, because I love you, too."

"I know."

"Yeah?"

"I've known for a while. And you're right." She chewed on her lower lip and he placed a delicate kiss there so she'd release her flesh before wounding it. "I was just too scared. I couldn't trust the idea that you might stay. I mean, there were signs everywhere, but my fears were like this giant shadow looming over everything…. I can't believe you didn't just pack up and leave, I was so…" She shuddered.

"You weren't that bad, Cass. You were going through a rough time." He traced her jaw with the pad of his thumb. "You were vulnerable."

She sighed.

"Besides, there were signs telling me to wait, be patient."

"There were?"

"You kept the truck."

She laughed.

"Wore my jersey to the game." He was holding her against him, which felt so right. He wanted to keep her forever, grow their family, celebrate everything in their lives together, mark everyone's height on the kitchen door frame. Even adopt a dog as crazy as PC was. "And you looked like you wanted to kill that fan outside the arena."

She laughed softly. "I did. I truly did."

"You trusted me to keep Dusty safe during that fire."

"You look out for him like he's your own flesh and blood."

"Family is—"

"—the people you choose."

He smiled. "And you let me see Dusty after his surgery."

"You didn't freak out when I called you his stepdad."

"Are you kidding? I was honored."

"Is Landon finally going to be my stepdad?" Dusty asked, popping around the corner.

Cass jumped, breaking contact with Landon. "How long have you been there?" she asked, her tone scolding, hands going to her hips.

Dusty's spine straightened, eyes wide. Silently, barely hiding a playful smirk, he sidestepped from the doorway and out of view.

Rylnn peeked into the room. "A long time. Lotta kissy-kissy." She vanished around the corner with a giggle.

Cass shook her head at Landon, her eyes narrowed as though outraged, but he could see she was trying to hide a grin. "I love those kids," she whispered.

Landon pulled her back into his arms. "So do I."

He gave her a long, slow kiss filled with love.

"Maybe when my season's over, you and I can sneak away for a weekend. Whaddya say?"

"Sign me up."

"Family trip!" Dusty announced, reappearing in the doorway. "Let's go to Legoland!"

Landon, laughing, kissed Cass again.

Family.

Not a better word in the world.

Although *wife* and *husband* were pretty good, too.

Maybe they could work on those next.

EPILOGUE

*H*olding hands with Landon, Cass walked down Main Street several weeks later during the town's first ever Armadillo Day. Violet went by in the Dragons costume, Daisy-Mae, her handler, nowhere in sight.

Cass saw Dylan O'Neill head into Blue Tumbleweed, and wondered whether Jenny and he had moved beyond texting and calling each other.

The two were like cats and dogs. Oil and water. Total opposites.

Kind of like Athena and Mullens. Cass had seen the two of them talking earlier, Athena looking impatient, Mullens trying to press a cup of hot cider into her hands before she hurried off to her bookshop and café.

Athena and her sister had put together a small float for the evening parade and they'd been giving out samples of their soon-to-be-famous huckleberry tarts. They must've made hundreds of the mini pies, all of which were gone before the parade reached the middle of town.

Cass had noticed that wherever Athena went tonight, Mullens seemed to appear, working hard to be helpful. So far, he'd received more eye rolls and dirty looks than the average man would tolerate. Why Athena hadn't yet chased him off was beyond Cass. Or why he hadn't given up yet. The man was a Casanova, not a bookworm like Athena wanted.

Those two were like Jenny and Dylan—oil and water. Total opposites.

Cass was glad to be out of the dating pool.

She leaned into Landon's shoulder, and he dropped a kiss on her forehead.

The kids were walking ahead of them down the cordoned-off street, checking out the various booths. The parade had finished, and the whole downtown was now a market, lit up by streetlights and extra strings of lights hanging criss-cross over the blocked off road. People could buy anything from armadillo teddy bears to cowboy hats and crocheted dishcloths, to takeout snacks or drinks from the lined-up food trucks.

Landon and Cass stopped beside Jenny's float, parked at the end of the street. To advertise her business she'd covered a flatbed trailer with fake snow, then positioned her store's mannequins under archways, wearing wedding gowns, prom dresses and Western wear.

Catching Cass studying the long, elegant wedding dress set at the back of the float, Landon said, "I picture you in something shorter."

"Because you love my legs?"

"Well, yes, but this one seems too... It would slow you down. You need something you can wear cowboy boots with, and can move in."

"Well, you're not gonna see me in anything like that unless you put a ring on it," she teased, holding up her bare ring finger.

He moved into her personal space, gently stroking the skin that an engagement ring would cover. "More importantly, would you like to feel a ring on this finger?"

"If it was from you, I might say yes."

"Might?" He pursed his lips, eyebrows raised.

"You'll never know unless you ask."

"It's way too soon." He began walking again,

and she hurried to keep up, surprised by his words.

"Is it though?" It felt as though they'd known each other a lot longer than a few months.

"What about the kids?" he asked seriously.

She glanced ahead, spotting them rooting through their bags of parade candy, swapping items with each other.

"Well," she said, equally seriously, "I think Rylnn would make a beautiful flower girl. Dusty a reliable ring-bearer."

Landon began laughing.

"I also happen to know this wedding venue where we could get a very good deal."

"Do you now?"

"They need a bit of experience. Sort of a dry run, if you know what I mean. But I hear they've already booked a local NHL celebrity and his beautiful fiancée."

"That's not us?"

"Not us." Cass glanced meaningfully toward Daisy-Mae, who was hustling through the crowd, clearly looking for someone.

"So we would be helping out this new business? Getting a deal in exchange for them doing a test-run wedding?"

Cass nodded.

"What sort of timeline are we thinking?" Landon asked.

"Before summer."

He nodded thoughtfully, his brow furrowed. "Once you decide to blast through your fears there's no stopping you, is there?"

"Am I moving too fast?" She felt a twinge of panic. She *was* moving really fast. But she'd never felt so sure about anything in her life as she did about Landon.

He gave her arm a reassuring squeeze. "We might be able to help them out."

Cass relaxed. Then her thoughts started whirling. Were they going to get married? So soon? There was so much work to do on the lodge before it would be ready.

Oh, who was she kidding? She could get married to Landon in the middle of a corral and she'd be happy.

They continued walking, moving past Athena's Huckleberry Bookshop, and the two sets of wrought-iron tables and chairs outside her large front windows. The door was propped open despite the cool January night, and Cass glanced inside, then stopped.

Landon continued on a few steps before realizing she was no longer with him. He came back to look through the open doorway of the shop as well.

Dusty and Rylnn raced past them and into the store. "Books!" they hollered.

"Slow down!" Cass scolded, fearing they might run into someone carrying a fresh cup of coffee.

"Mullens never struck me as a bookish type," Landon said, tipping his chin toward his teammate. The man was standing by a spinning rack near the front counter, his head buried in the pages of a book. Athena, ringing through someone's coffee order, kept glancing over at him.

"He's not...a professor type?" Cass asked breathlessly, barely daring to believe that it could be possible.

She and Landon shared an amused smile and snickered at the idea.

"Do you want to get married?" he asked quietly, leaning his shoulder against hers as they stood near the doorway. "I mean, I understand if you aren't open to the idea of trying again."

Cass gave him an incredulous look. "Are you serious?"

He nodded. Landon, ever the thoughtful man. And sometimes misguided by that thoughtfulness.

"I wasn't looking for the right sort of partner

the first time," she said, considering why she wasn't in the least bit gun-shy about marrying Landon. "But I've learned a lot since then. About myself." She leaned against him, tipping her lips up for a kiss. "And you. I love you. And I get the feeling that we could make a go of this. Successfully."

"We do make a pretty good team."

"No, we make an amazing team."

"In that case…" Landon pulled her away from the doorway and sat her in one of the wrought-iron chairs. Before she knew it, he was down on one knee, a ring box extended.

She didn't have to look around to know they were drawing attention.

She didn't care. She was already nodding.

Landon chuckled. "That's a good sign."

"Landon," Cass said, grabbing his hands. She ignored his look of alarm. "Landon Jackson, will you marry me? Will you make me the happiest woman this side of the Rio Grand? Will you be the man who matches my independence and makes me stronger and better just by being in my life? Will you be my second chance? Be more than my tool?"

"Cassandra McTavish, will *you* marry *me*? Will you make me the happiest man this side of the

Mississippi? Will you challenge me and make my life better in each and every way? Will you be the highlight of my day? Be more than my tool? Will you be my wife?"

She was nodding again, fumbling the ring from its box, helping him slide it onto her finger. She fell into his arms as he stood, hugging her tight. He kissed her wet cheeks, then her lips.

"I love you, Cass."

"I love you, too, Landon."

"So much kissy-kissy," Rylnn said, throwing herself into the hug.

"I happen to like kissy-kissy," Cass said.

"Me, too," Landon agreed, giving her another kiss.

"Can I pick your dress, Cassie?" Rylnn asked.

"You can help, but I get the final say," Cass answered, already imagining her soon-to-be stepdaughter in a flower-girl princess gown.

Rylnn thrust out her bottom lip, but Cass knew her pout wasn't real. But her son's joy sure was. He stood near Landon, smiling shyly.

"Hey, little man." Landon released Cass and bent down. "Are you okay with me marrying your mom?"

Dusty nodded, trying for the stoic cowboy

look and failing. Soon he was grinning and Landon was swinging him up and into his arms.

"Say cheese!"

Someone Cass recognized as working for the local online paper had a camera raised, waiting for them to turn his way. Landon settled Dusty on his hip, and Cass lifted Rylnn to her own. The little girl kissed her cheek as the photographer snapped a picture.

They set the children back down, and Rylnn took Dusty's hand, then Cass's. She instructed Dusty to take Landon's, lining them up for the cameraman, then commanded him to take another photo.

Once he had complied, she asked to see the photo and, apparently approving it, told him to email it to her parents.

Cass's heart swelled with happiness.

She looked at Landon, and saw that the dampness in his eyes matched her own.

"*Parents,*" he mouthed.

She gave a little nod, before turning with a smile as people gathered closer to offer their congratulations.

Then suddenly she was crashing into Landon as a loud, happy bark broke the air.

"Prince Charming!"

After jumping on her, the dog danced around them, barking, licking hands and slapping nearby well-wishers with his wagging tail.

Brant Wylder was futilely pulling on the end of PC's leash. "You wouldn't happen to want to re-foster him, would you? His new home didn't work out."

"No," Landon said, shaking his head and causing a chorus of moans from the kids, who had slung their arms around the Great Dane's neck and were being happily licked.

Cass opened her mouth to protest, but before she could speak, Landon told Brant, "No more fostering. We're adopting him."

With a grin, Brant handed over the leash and said something about two dogs, two NHLers, one night. But Cass didn't care because she was launching herself into Landon's arms, giving him a gigantic kiss.

ACKNOWLEDGMENTS

Thank you to Nate for naming Landon Jackson. When my name well runs dry you always help me out!

Also a big thank you to my Jeansters for weighing in on the dog's name when I realized I already had a doll named Maple in Falling for the Bodyguard and a donut place called Maples…and just called the dog Maple, too. Out of a variety of 'Brant names' they chose Stockdale for the great Dane Rylnn calls Prince Charming. (I never did share that Dusty likely finds that name disgusting!)

Thank you also goes to my team helping out behind the scenes with edits (Margaret Carney)—what do you mean Cass and Landon never actually started dancing at the gala? And Cass's purse is a no-show? Oh man… I'll fix that… (Except the detail about the purse. Just pretend it's there, okay? They're such a pain to deal with in real life, let's just pretend a fairy is holding it for her while she dances.) As well, thank you to my beta readers (Donna W., Erika H., Margaret C., Sharon S. and Lucy J.). You rock! Thank you as well to my error team who see the book last and remind me that Cass might still be wearing that tiara… Yeah, I'll change that as well—thanks Audrey B.!

And finally, thank you to everyone who reads my stories and laughs and cries and feels "all the feels" was my daughter would say. I hope you enjoy Cass and Landon's story and that it makes you feel good.

HOCKEY SWEETHEARTS: HAVE YOU READ THEM ALL?

The Cupcake Cottage

Peach Blossom Hollow

Chocolate Cherry Cabin

The Peppermint Lodge

The Huckleberry Bookshop

Sugar Cookie Country House

The Gingerbread Cafe

There are two more series set in Sweetheart Creek!

The Cowboys of Sweetheart Creek, Texas

The Cowboy's Stolen Heart (Levi)

The Cowboy's Secret Wish (Myles)

The Cowboy's Second Chance (Ryan)

The Cowboy's Sweet Elopement (Brant)

The Cowboy's Surprise Return (Cole)

Indigo Bay

Sweet Matchmaker (Ginger and Logan)

Sweet Holiday Surprise (Cash & Alexa)

Sweet Forgiveness (Ashton & Zoe)
Sweet Troublemaker (Nick & Polly)
Sweet Joymaker (Maria & Clint)

MORE SMALL TOWN ROMANCES BY JEAN ORAM…

Veils and Vows

The Promise (Book 0: Devon & Olivia)

The Surprise Wedding (Book 1: Devon & Olivia)

A Pinch of Commitment (Book 2: Ethan & Lily)

The Wedding Plan (Book 3: Luke & Emma)

Accidentally Married (Book 4: Burke & Jill)

The Marriage Pledge (Book 5: Moe & Amy)

Mail Order Soulmate (Book 6: Zach & Catherine)

Blueberry Springs

Whiskey and Gumdrops (Mandy & Frankie)

Rum and Raindrops (Jen & Rob)

Eggnog and Candy Canes (Katie & Nash)

Sweet Treats (3 short stories—Mandy, Amber, & Nicola)

Vodka and Chocolate Drops (Amber & Scott)

Tequila and Candy Drops (Nicola & Todd)

Champagne and Lemon Drops (Beth & Oz)

ABOUT THE AUTHOR

Jean Oram is a *New York Times* and *USA Today* best-selling romance author. Inspiration for her small town series came from her own upbringing on the Canadian prairies. Although, so far, none of her characters have grown up in an old schoolhouse or worked on a bee farm. Jean still lives on the prairie with her husband, two kids, and big shaggy dog where she can be found out playing in the snow or hiking.

Become an Official Fan:
www.facebook.com/groups/jeanoramfans

Newsletter: www.jeanoram.com/signup
Website & blog: www.jeanoram.com

Find a complete, up-to-date book list at:
www.jeanoram.com/books